Searching for

# Higher Ground

# Searching for
# Higher Ground

A Novel

by

## Steve Josse

An Inspirational Adventure Story

In Memory of John Denver

*This book is dedicated
to John Denver
for the inspiration his music
gave me and countless others.*

## Higher Ground

*There are those who can live with the things they
don't believe in. They are giving their lives for
something less than it can be. Some have longed
for a place in inspiration – some will fill the
emptiness inside by giving it all – for the things
that they believe. Maybe it's a dream in me, maybe
it's just my style. Maybe it's just freedom that I've
found – but given the possibility of living up to the
dream in me, you know that I'll be reaching for
Higher Ground.*

*by John Denver and Joe Henry*

In Appreciation:

*My editor, Shelley Blumberg*

*My dear friends for their loving support*

*Gail Buck*
*Lorelei Dacus*
*David Feinstein*
*Elizabeth Nardi*
*Jane Wendell*

# Introduction

"It's going to be up to the women in this country to show their feminine side and say it's okay to love and care for one another. Women, it's time that you stand up and say 'bullshit' to all the wars, violence, poverty, overpopulation, and greed. We need to take the best of both sexes – to offer and combine them instead of just relying on masculine traits – to guide us.

"Somehow, through the ages, I think the best that women have had to offer – the feminine traits of love, compassion, and faith – has often been overruled and overshadowed by fear and greed. It's time we take these positive traits and make them the basis of our new society – our new family and community units. Remember we are ONE; we're all in this together, and so let's act together.

"This afternoon we shall start to rebuild Watts, and tomorrow we shall rebuild the rest of the country, if for no other reason than for the sake of our children. We must try to be what we hope our children will become. If we're not there to be positive role models, who will be? May peace be with you. Thank you."

– Excerpt from President Deborah Mandell's speech
Watts, California; May 11, 2012

# Chapter 1

I lie flat on my back across my single bed with my head dangling out the window. Hopelessly, I try to count the thousands of drops of rain as they madly rush against my face and into my open mouth. As I wipe the dampness out of my eyes, a single morning star plays peek-a-boo through a veil of wildly dancing clouds – allowing time for one quick wish before my rain-filled eyes again must close. In a time of so much turmoil, what can I do but make a wish for peace?

Pulling my drenched head back through the open window, I stretch out on the bed. My body quivers; goose bumps parade over my bare chest. Though I pull my down comforter up and curl my feet around its end, warmth, it seems, will not come easily.

The radio commentator keeps talking about a collapse being imminent; the chills keep running up my spine. In a somber voice he announces that – after several days of speculation whether she would even accept the office – "New President Deborah Mandell was sworn in this morning at 9 a.m. EST. Her first official act as President was to declare a state of national emergency.

"Within an hour of that act the governors of New York and Rhode Island joined California in declaring martial law." His voice picks up speed. "The New York Stock Market has fallen another 120 points today, dropping below 2,000 for the first time in over thirty years. The Stock Exchange was shut down. . ."

My stomach feels queasy and restless. My mind insists on racing through all the possible scenarios. I reach over and switch off my radio-phone.

Rolling off the air-bed, I walk into the bathroom and take a quick, steamy hot shower. Grabbing a fluffy blue towel, I rub my curly black hair hard and try to figure out how all this could be happening. How can a nation disintegrate right in front of our very eyes, and its people seem helpless to stop it?

Sticking my head back out my window, first light now plays hopscotch through the mist and broken showers. I can see the orange tip of the sun flirting with the crest of the mountains after making its morning pilgrimage up and over the snowcapped peaks of the Wallowas. Looking across the meadow, I see a group of about twenty men and women from our community. Dressed in rain slickers in a variety of colors and styles, they form a ragged circle on the wet grass below my room. One by one they join hands.

Philip, a fellow of about my own age wearing a bright yellow rainsuit but no hat, turns his soggy blond head, looks up at my window, cocks his head, and smiles. Gently, he pulls his left hand from the clasp of the woman on his left, raises it above his head and waves it back and forth.

As I wave back, the first smile of the morning breaks over my face. Philip then turns his palms straight up. I can read his mouth mimicking the question: "Why, Jason, are you still in your room?"

My name is Jason Mann. I am twenty years old and, along with my father, have lived most of my life in Higher Ground, an intentional community of approximately 3,700 people who live in the high plateau country of Eastern Oregon. Our community was founded by a small group of social planners in the late 1990s. By that time, according to my father, the handwriting was already on the wall – the U.S. and much of the world were entering into the chaotic period that was to close out the 20th Century. The original planners of Higher Ground felt that we needed to come up with a whole new plan, that our old way of living wasn't working any more. They decided we needed to learn how to live with one another in a loving, caring manner – one based on cooperation instead of competition, love instead of fear – and learn how to use our intuition as our guide instead of just our heads. It's a very simple philosophy, one that at that time some thought rather naive and unobtainable. But it's a philosophy we've proven works, one that changes one's lifestyle totally – if followed.

Now it's time to share what we have lived. Many people seem to think a collapse of American society is imminent, that only a miracle can save it. We hope to be a small part of that miracle.

I turn away from the window and walk over to the large dresser at the far end of the room. No one seems to know how long we'll be gone, so I have packed as much as will fit in my two medium-sized, antique suitcases. I have to kneel on the brown one to get the latch to lock.

A suitcase in each hand, I walk the seven steps to my bedroom door, then stop, turn around and take one last look. My room is small, about ten feet by twelve. The walls are cream-colored adobe, and the concrete floor is dominated by a large Nez Perce rug. An airbed with my warm down comforter, my radio-phone, a brown dresser and a desk with my computer is about all that space allows. The pictures I have painted and photographs of my friends all remind me of what I will miss the most.

In the silence I can hear the rain on the roof. Inside my room it's warm and cozy; outside looks cold, wet, and uninviting. I have been safe and loved here, my existence one of peace and security. Today I will leave all this and, along with other community volunteers from all over the nation, go to what was once called the City of Angels to see if we can be of help in this year 2012.

It takes an entire village
to raise a child.

African Proverb

# Chapter 2

I count twenty-seven other community members boarding this ancient diesel bus ahead of me. One by one, we hand our bags to Bob, our driver, who sticks them into the dark cavern underneath our silver and maroon relic.

"Good morning, Jason. You about ready to head south?" Bob asks. "I'd like to make it off this High Desert by nightfall. Hear there's some heavier weather coming in, maybe some spring snow. At seventy-one, I don't much like putting chains on anymore."

"I'm as ready as I'll ever be," I respond as I get in line behind Melissa, who at 16 is the youngest of our group.

"Morning, Jason," Melissa says as she gives me a warm hug. "This trip is kinda scary," she adds with a half smile, then turns around and moves on into the bus.

I pause on the second step and let my eyes scan what I can see of our community nestled between evergreen covered bluffs. I take in a deep breath of pine and listen to the gurgling of Little Fawn Creek as it gushes down a steep boulder-covered ravine next to our lot. I am going to miss this place.

I wave one last time to my father, who is standing among about a hundred well-wishers gathered around the bus.

He has a relaxed smile on his bearded face — as if I were leaving for just a weekend camping trip. That's my dad for sure, looking so calm and in control. He takes his hands out of his gray wool coat and waves back. "Jason, you take care. "I love you. See you in a couple of months."

It seems like I've spent a fair amount of time lately wondering why he and my mom split up. He never talks about her much. He says she is a nice lady, but that they were going in different directions. The last time I heard from her was about three years ago and she was in L. A.

Making my way down the narrow aisle, Jess grabs my hand, "Jason, glad you're coming. We need some young blood on this trip." Laughingly, I tell him that I *think* I'm glad too, but I'll tell him for sure in a couple of months.

"Hey, Jason," says Naomi as we slap hands. "Was wondering if you'd ever leave Higher Ground! I'm happy you're jumping out of the nest, and that we're going down south together. This should be quite an adventure!"

"I think so! Glad you're going too, Naomi. You never know when I may need a pretty older woman to hold my hand down there." I look back at her as I go by; she just smiles and rolls her eyes.

Three empty seats in the middle of the bus catch my attention. Stuffing my two suitcases in the compartment above my head, I grab a worn looking seat next to a dirt-stained window. I see Philip scurrying up to the steps of the bus, an overstuffed suitcase in each hand and a large green duffel bag roped around his neck. Blue silk boxer shorts dangle out the side of one suitcase and the other one is tied together with what looks like yellow rope.

"I was wondering, Jason, if you were coming," says Philip as he strains to make his large green duffel bag fit underneath our tan naugahyde seats. "You didn't make group. Thought you might have changed your mind – decided this adventure was a little too much for an intellectual type like yourself."

I look over at Philip, just smile and shake my head. Philip hasn't changed much over the fifteen years we've been best friends. With his shaggy blond hair, puppy dog eyes and a grin an acre in diameter, he looks no different to me now at nineteen than when he was ten.

"Hey," I tell him, "I was just taking my time. Gotta admit I was a little nervous when I first got up this morning and heard that the New York Stock Exchange had shut down again, and that angry customers were rioting outside. But heck, that seems to be life in 21st Century America. I'm fine now. How about you? Any second thoughts?"

"No way. I am ready to roll," laughs Philip, his patented grin sprawled across his face. "This is going to be the biggest adventure of my life, and I am ready. I need some excitement in my life and I think this is going to be it. Why, just think of all those pretty girls down there in Southern California I haven't even met yet. They're going to fall all over us Oregon boys coming down there to help them out. I can't wait."

"Right, Philip. You've always made an impression on the girls. That's for sure. But I thought that was the problem: too many girls in love with you, not enough time, spreading yourself too thin. What're you going to do when you get to the big city and you have half a million unmarried women running around?"

"Don't know," says Philip. His smile spans epic proportions as he reclines his seat back in a full rest position. "But its going to be fun trying to figure it all out."

"Great!" I answer. "Like we weren't going to have our hands full already!"

"Hey Jason, cheer up. You look like you've just lost your best friend. And here I am, sitting right next to you, alive and well. Hey look! We're finally moving; we're on our way to adventure!"

Sure enough, we're moving. We wind our way through rows of electric cars and vans that fill our parking lot, but our bus doesn't go 200 feet when Bob brakes and we come to a momentary halt. A brown doe, her white rump in the air, and two small spotted fawns cross the road in front of us. They pay us little attention as they playfully meander along, nibbling at the tender shoots of early spring grass along our gravel road. The doe is Maggie; I can tell by the way her ears flop to the side of her head. She's been living here in our nature preserve for at least five years that I can remember. Laura, one of our naturopaths, found her in the National Forest about five miles east of here, next to the butchered carcass of her mother. Laura bottle fed her until she was old enough to join our resident herd, and she's been here ever since, always seeming to have perpetual twins following her about.

Bob lightly presses down on the accelerator. We're moving along at less than the fifteen-mile speed limit, skirting the edge of our homes. We have green common spaces filled with parks and playgrounds where most communities have streets. We do have feeder roads around our perimeter, but only bicycles and electric carts can enter the interior.

We pass over the wooden bridge on Hurricane Creek, the water's pace now slowed by the flatness of the valley floor. Boulders taller than my lanky six foot frame are scattered among the river rock that lines the 80-foot wide bed of the stream. Three years ago, in the spring of 09, the water raged down, cresting the creek at almost 20 feet. We lost nineteen older style, stick frame houses. But the homes that were made out of what we call stress skin panels, which are large panels of recycled polyurethane sandwiched between strain board, were so strong that they didn't budge.

It was the worst flood ever recorded in Wallowa County. But in the 28 days that followed, all the homes were rebuilt and several hundred trees replanted. I think virtually every person in the community did something to help. The elderly baked cookies for the crews that did the house raising.

Children planted trees, craftsmen built new furniture, and musicians played their music at the fund raising events. It was like the community decided losing the homes was an good excuse for a month long festival.

After crossing the creek, our road runs alongside our business district, with its old-fashioned buildings and cobblestone walkways. The original founders of the community decided that even though we were using ecologically innovative building techniques in construction, we should still give the whole downtown an old Tudor village look, with a public square, and pedestrian-only streets.

I smile when I notice Goodies, our yogurt and candy store. Through the openings in the stained glass window I can see  Margaret Melloncamp moving around. She must be getting ready to open up. I can remember when she and her husband Larry first opened their business – everyone in the community seemed so excited.

I must have been eight or nine years old when my dad took me to Goodies and bought me a shake with strawberries fresh from our community garden. That day stands out as perhaps the highlight of the whole year. We sat at a shiny new table drinking our shakes, my dad being his usual self and not saying much. But I could almost touch the feeling of love that came from him and the whole group of people who had gathered to celebrate the Grand Opening that day. It gave me such a feeling of security – a feeling I've also experienced so many times at the meals that we share each week or at our work parties, at school and at our weekly gatherings. It's a security I've carried with me my entire life, knowing that I am an integral part of my village, that I have a large support system of people who truly care.

"Well," says Philip, breaking my train of thought, "that's about it. I see the main highway up ahead. Now we're really on our way."

Our bus comes down the hill to a full stop. Sage and juniper cover the sprawling hills and valleys below us for as far as I can see. A green sign no larger than a mailbox reads "Klamath Falls – 234 Miles." Bob turns the bus to the west as he pulls onto the main highway, a large gray asphalt river that will carry us as it meanders its way through Eastern Oregon, down through Central California, into Southern California, and on to what I am sure will be the biggest adventure of my life.

# Chapter 3

The jarring and moaning of the bus stopping at Klamath Falls' first stoplight wakes Phil. He stares at me blurry eyed and mutters, "Are we here yet?"

"Are we *where?*" I ask, looking over at him skeptically.

"In L.A. – the City of Angels, the place where all the babes are," he answers as he stretches his arms above his head and yawns.

"In L.A.? Are you serious? We haven't even gone two hundred miles yet. We've still got over seven hundred miles to go."

"Oh." Philip shrugs as he curls back up in his seat. "Wake me up when we get there, okay? Good night."

"Come on, Philip," I prod as I gently shake his shoulder. "We're pulling into a restaurant. Let's get something to eat and check this place out."

"Do I have to?" Philip slowly sits up and wipes the sleep out of his eyes. "Okay," he says with a thin smile as he looks at my frowning face. "Let's see what the world looks like outside Higher Ground."

Everyone except Bob is out the bus door before I can get Philip moving. Bob stops us at the door, smiles kindly, and tells us to watch our step – that this is a different world than Higher Ground, that people are acting a little crazy. "And keep your eye on your wallets," he adds. "I had mine picked my last trip out." We thank Bob for the advice as we step out the door onto a deserted parking lot that seems to have more potholes than pavement.

Philip stands with his arms folded and looks around at the trash-filled, almost empty lot. Then he glances across the street at the abandoned-looking bank building and at a group of cold looking folk milling about the front. "Jason, what are we doing here? What have you got me into? What have I gotten *you* into?" I just stare back at him and shake my head, not even giving him the satisfaction of a reply.

We walk in the front door of a Denny's restaurant; the aroma of French fries mingles with a subdued aura. The peeling wallpaper and the dirty yellow and brown commercial carpet give the place a worn out feeling. The place must have been virtually empty before our group walked in, and now the two waitresses are scurrying about in a state of what looks like near panic.

Philip scans the scene and seems to spy an empty seat at a table with several of our younger female members. He taps me on the shoulder and points. "I'll be right over there if you need me." I shake my head, look around, and then head for an empty seat in a corner booth as Irene, Marv, and Melissa wave me over.

Our waitress – still breathing hard – finally makes it over to our table. She is a tall, stout, redheaded gal with large green, tired-looking eyes, a rather short skirt and (I can't help but notice) long, tan legs. She introduces herself as Karen and hands each of us a red plastic-covered menu.

As I hold my menu up, I see large globs of what looks like brown gravy glued to the plastic. Karen, her face gathering a slight peach color, looks over at me, winks and laughs lightly. "There's no charge for the gravy young man. It comes with the meal. I'm really glad to have some customers," she continues. "It's been months since we've seen a busload of people in here. Where are you folks going?"

We look at one another, all of us seemingly hesitant to answer. Finally, Irene (the senior person both at the table and on our trip, having just turned 70) answers in her slow North Carolina drawl. "We're on our way to Southern California." With that, Irene props her elbow on the table and puts her chin on her knuckles as if waiting patiently for the next question.

"Oh my," says Karen with a surprised look on her face and with her hands on her hips. "I hear things are really bad down there. You couldn't pay me enough to even cross that California border. It's bad news, real bad news. I can't imagine why anybody would want to go down there nowadays.

"You know, most people around *here* left from down *there.* Ain't much work up here since the last of the mills shut down last week but at least the trouble wasn't so bad, until just lately. Now those mill workers are so mad, they're causing all kinds of problems. My Uncle Bob worked there 32 years when they laid him off. The employees wanted to buy the mill from the stockholders, but the owners decided it was more profitable to dismantle it and sell it piecemeal. Now they're supposed to bring in some scab workers to tear it apart since the local workers won't do it. You folks watch your step if you're going to walk around town. Those people across the street are family folks and they're okay, but you go down the street by the mill entrance and they're a mad bunch.

"Anyway, you people have such good manners and look so nice. When the first ones in your group walked through the door and saw we were understaffed – that is for a bunch your size – they just pitched in and helped us set up tables. Now, why would nice folks like you want to go to California at a time like this?"

My stomach is already starting to feel queasy and I am not sure what to say, so I look over at tall, lanky silver haired

Marv who, at age 65, is one of my mentors. He just slowly smiles at me, raises his eyebrows slightly and then looks over at Irene.

"We're going down to L.A. to do a job," answers Irene concisely, but with a friendly mysterious grin on her face. She doesn't say another word, just keeps resting her chin on her knuckles.

Karen hesitates, as if waiting for her to say more. When it's obvious she won't, Karen says, "Well, everybody to their own thing. You guys are awfully brave, that's all I can say." She smiles again weakly and heads to the next table.

"People around here sure seem nervous," Melissa says as she fidgets with her spoon and looks around the room. "It's like fear is hanging over this town like a swarm of locusts over a field of wheat. I can feel it all the way down to my bones."

"Unfortunately, fear is what motivates most people in our society," Irene says matter-of-factly. "When times get tough, fear feeds on fear and chaos reigns. That seems to be where much of the world is right now."

"It's the same old Survival-of-the-Fittest ethic that has ruled the world since the beginning of time," says Marv as he looks at Melissa and me, his face solemn and serious. "It's that 'I-won't-have-enough-if-you-get-yours' attitude. No country in the history of the world has ever had the riches this country had and still has. There has always been enough for everyone here. It's just about distributing it more equally, and that's where the fear comes in."

"I understand that," says Melissa, still playing with her spoon. "I realize my mom and I just moved to Higher Ground from the sticks of Colorado, and I guess I am still a novice at all this, but that's not the way we act at the community. Why are we so different?"

"Melissa, this is what you young folks are going to learn about on this trip," interjects Irene. "How at our communities we've tried to do things differently, and with some success — sometimes very good success. We take it for granted that everyone in our community is assured of a job, food, shelter, medical coverage and childcare; that our basic needs are met without having to stress all the time, which leaves so much more time to be creative and adventurous. But that's not the way it is out here in the rest of the world."

"Yea, I can see that," mutters Melissa. "People really do seem stressed out here."

Marv looks around at the rest of our community members scattered about the restaurant, "You know, it's the same with the love we have for one another. It's there all the time unconditionally; we're always focusing on it. We don't have to waste so much time searching for it. When we replace fear with love, it frees us to be our real selves to find more joy and happiness.

"But you, Jason, have to remember you were practically born into this way of life; it wasn't always this way. We've had to work hard at it. It's taken a long time to come into fruition. It's going to be a real education for you kids to see how much of the rest of the world lives."

"Sorry to interrupt you guys," says Karen as she walks up to our table balancing a tray of dishes. "You look pretty intent in whatever you're talking about."

*Intense, not intent,* I think to myself; that's the word. My stomach feels rather uneasy, and I find I have lost much of my appetite. I eat only half of my fish sandwich, and I get up from the table. As I do so, Irene looks over at me; her eyelids raised, she gives me an empathic smile. I give her a tight smile back, excuse myself, walk to the front entrance of the coffee shop and peer out the glass door.

The sky is still overcast and the thermometer on the empty U.S. Bank building across the highway reads 37 degrees. I know my friends wonder what I am doing, but I am not sure myself. We have grown up using our intuition and insights. I feel like I am supposed to be doing *some*thing, though I am not sure exactly what.

As I stare out the door, my attention is focused on a group of what looks like homeless people standing in front of a Safeway supermarket. I had noticed them earlier when Philip and I walked in the coffee shop. They look cold as they walk back and forth, their hands stuffed in their pockets, their breath floating through the air. The dampness in the air makes it feel colder than it is. I feel a chill run down my spine just watching them. I turn around, politely raise my voice, and tell my friends at the table I will be back in just a couple of minutes. Without waiting for a reply, I open the door, walk out into the drizzling rain, and immediately head across the near empty, four-lane highway.

From out the window of the coffee shop I had been noticing one family in particular, standing apart from the others. There's a man who looks in his mid-forties, unshaven, and dressed in a patched pair of jeans and an old green army jacket with an emblem of a horse on the side. On his feet are what looks like a pair of brown cowboy boots with what (even from this distance) looks like a large hole in the left toe.

As I get to the sidewalk, maybe ten feet away, I notice his thin face houses friendly blue eyes. So I feel only a little hesitation as I go over, stand in front of him, and introduce myself.

"Hi. My name is Jason, Jason Mann. I was eating breakfast across the street, and I couldn't help noticing you folks standing out in the cold. I am not sure there's much I can do to help, and I don't mean to insult you, but here's $5.00." I take a $5 bill out of my wallet and hold it out in front of me. "Maybe it will help a little," I add looking at the man with uncertainty and now more than a little uneasiness.

The man stares intently at me with his light blue eyes for several seconds, seconds that seem like several minutes. I begin to wonder if he is insulted, but then he puts out his callused left hand, takes my money, and slowly looks at it as if checking to see if it is real. Then he reaches with his right hand for mine, and we firmly shake hands.

"I am glad to meet you, Jason," he says in a low, gentle voice. "My name is Jed Carlson, and this here is my wife, Trudy, and my two sons, Josh and Jessie. We appreciate your $5 – we really do. I guess it's just a little hard to take money from a stranger, especially one so young. We'd been hoping to find someone who could give us some work this morning, but no luck yet. But this five'll buy us a gallon of milk and a loaf of bread."

I look over at Trudy, a thin, small brunette in a tattered, printed cotton dress and a worn Levi jacket. She smiles rather quickly, looks me in the eye briefly, and says, "Hi. We really do appreciate the money." Then her eyes dive for the pavement below.

The two boys, who look to be about ten and twelve, both say, "Howdy," and shake my hand politely, staring up at me with wide-open eyes. Feeling much relief and to break the ice, I ask, "Where you folks from? It's obvious these two boys – with their Levi jackets, cowboy boots, and Wrangler jeans – are cowboys."

Jed smiles, showing his broken upper front teeth and empty gums on the bottom. "Yeah, we've lived and worked on ranches since before the boys were hatched. We lived in and around Burns, about 150 miles east of here, for about twelve years. This on-again, off-again drought got us though. Half as many cows out there now as there were ten years ago, so half as much work. Was up in Bend a couple of weeks ago but couldn't find work there either. With that darn ski area closed most of the winter and not enough water for all those golf courses, tourists just aren't coming in. It's gotten mighty lean around this part of the country."

"Where do you guys go at night? Where do you live?" I ask, not looking forward to the answer.

"Well, we've got us an old army tent outside town down by the Klamath River." As Jed talks his shoulders seem to drop before my eyes. "There are close to 200 of us... you might say *semi-retired* folks living down there. We walk back there every night. We need to get these kids in school, but the school district won't let them in without a permanent address." He adds, now talking faster and more urgently. "Don't like to leave these kids down there all day by themselves; things get a little rough down there at times. So, here we are. At least we'll be heading into summer in another month. It'll be a little warmer and, hopefully, some farm work will be available." Jed rubs his gloveless hands together and stomps his feet.

We continue to talk for another ten minutes about their life and the state of the country when I hear someone yell, "Hey, Jason. It's time to go." I look across the street and see Bob in front of the bus shouting at me.

I'm at a loss for words. What do I say to this family – destitute, with no real place to live, and the opportunity for a job relatively bleak? I again feel a little sick to my stomach, but I manage to shake Jed's hand and, with a washed-out smile, I wish them all the best of luck. Each one of them (almost as in a trance) thanks me and wishes me the same.

I turn and run back across the highway to the safety of our bus. I am the last one aboard. Bob looks straight ahead and doesn't say a word as I climb the stairway and quietly walk past him through the bus, two dozen eyes giving me support and several people touching my hand. I end up in the back of the bus feeling like I'm in shock and sit down in an empty seat behind Philip.

The bus heads down the main drag and Phil turns around, concern engraved on his face. "You okay?"

26

"I dunno. Those folks I just talked to, the Carlsons, they are a nice family. What are they doing living on the street?"

"Yeah they looked all right to me," Phil says. "Look, there's another larger group on the next corner by the light." They look like all men and a little rougher bunch. I wonder if those are the mill workers I heard Karen talking about.

Suddenly, as we stop at the red light, several of the men reach into their coat pockets and take out what looks like handfuls of rocks. One of the men with a long dark coat and a face that could be out of a Charles Dickens novel arches his arm and throws a large rock at our bus. I see another shorter heavier man do the same. *Crack!* A rock hits the bus. *Crack!* Another thump and then the shattering of glass.

There is no one sitting next to me, so I quickly dive across my seat. There must be four or five rocks that actually hit the windows. *Jesus!* I say to myself. *We're being attacked!* Poking my head around my seat I look down the aisle and see at least two of the windows broken. Several of our group members are covered with shattered glass. I can hear people yelling and screaming, "Scabs! Scabs!"

I start to sit up, to see what is happening, when the bus starts violently rocking back and forth and then starts leaning dangerously to the left side. I hear a women scream, and then Philip yells that they're trying to tip us over!

Suddenly the bus takes off with a jolt and I'm thrown back against my seat. Bob presses down on the accelerator and we go through the red light... and maybe one or two more. It's hard to tell, lying across my seat. Bob just keeps driving without slowing or stopping until, I guess, he figures we're safe, now that we're on the outskirts of town.

One by one, we start sitting back up in our seats. No one is saying a word. Melissa (who was sitting across the aisle and is covered with broken glass) doesn't seem to want to sit back up. She lies across her seat, her tear-filled brown eyes like giant saucers looking across at me.

"Mel, are you okay?" asks Dr. Ron after he crawls on his hands and knees down the aisle to her.

"No, Doc, I don't think I am all right. I'm not bleeding, but I can't stop shaking. What was that all about? We didn't do anything to them. Why'd they attack us?" Tears stream uncontrollably down her face. No one seems to know what to say.

Irene comes over, sits next to her and wraps her arms around Melissa's shoulder while Dr. Ron picks the glass out of Mel's long straight brown hair. Both of them try to reassure her that everything's okay.

I look around. We're all stunned. The physical damage looks slight, but the psychological disillusionment seems much greater.

"Folks," Bob says rapidly into his microphone, "I hope everyone back there is okay. I'm going to keep driving until I can find a place I feel is safe. We'll stop and find some cardboard to put in the broken windows. I think it would be a good idea to form a group and talk about what just happened."

We drive out of Klamath Falls for another fifteen or twenty miles. Bob pulls the bus into a long space reserved for trucks at a rest stop. Everyone is quiet. Even Bob, who has been giving us the tour guide narrative the whole trip, is now quiet and subdued. The rest stop has only a few cars. It's not raining this far south; however, I am sure the local farmers wish it were. There's been enough moisture though, for the grass under the trees to start turning green, and it looks inviting.

No one needs to give directions. Without speaking, one by one we file out of the bus and form a circle on the grass. There is a slight breeze blowing, and the clouds seem to have magically disappeared. We sit next to one another in a circle and hold hands for five minutes. Still, no one speaks.

Finally Jess – who is a tall, lean gray-haired man near 65, one of the original members of our community – breaks the silence. "Many of you younger ones have spent little time outside our community. You've had little experience in seeing how the outside world lives. What you've seen today is just the beginning. As we travel further south, things will only get worse. There is much fear out here. People are feeling desperate and trapped. Most of you have not had to deal with fear. Most of the time it is absent from our community. Now many of us are feeling it for the first time, others for the first time in many years. How we deal with this may well decide if our journey is to be successful. I can only ask that you replace fear with faith in what we're attempting to do – to focus on what we want to have happen and not on what we fear or don't want. Then let go and let God or the universe take charge. If we can do that, we will be successful; it's Universal Law and it works."

Jess is quiet. Silence settles in again. In the distance the only sound is a whippoorwill singing his call that early spring is once again upon us.

Naomi, sitting to my left, is the next one to break the silence. In her early twenties, she is a sensitive, vibrant, outspoken woman with short brown hair and large brown eyes that are soft as a doe's. She has lived in our community since its inception. She is known for her wisdom and humor – both highly regarded characteristics in our community. Naomi's face is rose-colored as she speaks with great emotion. A tear runs down her cheek.

"I am certainly scared. I can remember being scared as a child when I lived outside our community. I don't like this feeling. It doesn't feel natural to me any more. When we decided to go on this journey, we talked about the hardships we would face. By consensus, we decided we should go. We know we must do what we can to help if any of us in the world are to survive. We cannot live in a vacuum, separate from the rest of the world any longer. What's happening out there is creeping into our communities. From this moment on we must turn our hearts to complete love for the people who suffer across the land. We must live as we have in the community, with faith. We must help make the reality of others' lives center on love, prosperity, and peace. From this moment we should strike fear from our hearts and go ahead as one – as we are one, all of us here and all of us out there."

Another silence descends. I feel a calmness come over me, connected again to my friends. Nothing else needs to be said. Without spoken words, we each pray or meditate. It matters not which religion, if any, we practice. We have Catholics, New Thoughters, Presbyterians, Jews, Buddhists, and Agnostics among us. It matters not. We are all one and our hearts know this to be true.

Rising, one by one we walk quietly back into the bus. I feel physically exhausted. Sitting for long periods of time makes me tired, and the violence in Klamath Falls has drained me. I start to walk down the aisle when I notice Philip sitting by himself, looking out the window with a faraway look in his eyes.

"You want any company?" I ask. "You look a little lonely."

"Sure," says Phil in an uneven voice. "Sit down for a while, Jason. I haven't talked to you since we left Klamath Falls. We've been gone barely five hours and already it seems like we left a month ago."

"I agree," I say as I sit down next to him, stretching my long legs out in front of me. "I'm just glad we're going down south together, Philip," I tell him honestly. "I'm a little nervous about this whole adventure, especially after what just happened in Klamath Falls. What do you think? You still ready for an adventure?"

"I'm okay, Jason." Phil's smile looks forced. "But I'm feeling a bit overwhelmed. That was some crazy deal! I see all of these people here in the world outside Higher Ground, and they live so differently than we do. It just seems so chaotic out here."

"I know what you mean. It's like everybody out here is doing their own thing regardless of how it affects other people. I mean, when I was in Klamath Falls talking to the Carlsons – who have no place to live and nothing to eat – up drives this guy and this woman in this big gas-guzzling, black Cadillac that probably cost them $50,000 bucks. You know, Phil, they drove by real slow and just looked over at us like we were in a zoo and that we were nothing, I mean absolutely nothing. I guess they just assumed I was one of the homeless. Then they speeded up and kept driving and never looked back."

"It's crazy, Philip. I know some people in Bend are living in houses costing a million bucks and big enough to house fifty people; others don't have any place to live and are going hungry. It just doesn't make any sense to me."

"You're right." Philip sounds uncharacteristically bitter. "Survival of the Fittest just doesn't fit into a modern culture anymore. Einstein said the way we live and react to the world is determined by whether we regard the world as a friendly place. Well, it doesn't look too friendly to me out here, so no wonder people are paranoid. I mean, it's like the whole system out here is antiquated. It needs to be redone and completely redefined.

"Jason, do you remember back in primary school? I guess we were about twelve, and Karen Kindrex was our teacher. You and I got in a real big argument; I don't even remember about what. For days afterwards we said that we actually hated each other. Finally, Karen got so sick of us arguing that she took us out of class and put us under a tree in the parkway. She told us not to come back to class until we had talked things out. You remember that?"

"I remember it well," I answer. "Within an hour we were great friends again, and I don't think we've ever had a big argument since. Now we always talk things out before they get big."

"Exactly, Jason. You've got it. That's what the rest of this crazy world needs to do. Take time, sit under a tree together every day, relax and talk things out. Put himself or herself in the other person's place. Realize that we're all in this together. That's all we've got to teach, Jason. That's all."

"I hope it's that simple, I really do." I stand up feeling a heavy burden on my shoulders and doubts in my mind. I put my hand on Philip's shoulder. "Let's get some sleep. I'll grab the empty seat in the back where I can lie down. I'll see you when we wake up in California." I lean over and give Philip a hug, feeling much more connected, and head to the back of the bus.

# Chapter 4

Ten-thirty. The dim light above my head makes me strain to see my watch. I must have been asleep when we entered California. Slept for nearly five hours. I try to focus and look about; most everyone else already looks awake. I see we are pulling into a large bus depot. Must be downtown Sacramento as that is our only listed stop. The station looks old. The architectural style reminds me of pictures of buildings of the 1930's. Large cracks run from the floor to the ceiling of the concrete depot. Trash lies everywhere. The place seems to be dying. I see no other buses, just an almost empty building. Bob tells us we need to get some diesel, and then we'll be on our way in about twenty minutes.

As we pull up to the unloading platform, the damp smell of decay fills the air. Out the window, I notice about a dozen young people my age sitting or lying down on benches in the depot lobby, their belongings in canvas bags that they hold in their laps or use as pillows. They look tired and dirty, like they have been working or living outside for a long time. As we get close, I can see that they're all black. Their faces look tired and drained of life's energy, like porcelain statues – not talking or moving, just staring at us as we pull in.

Naomi, sitting in the first row, must have noticed this group too for as soon as the bus comes to a complete stop, she is up and out the door. With her hands stuffed in her jeans, she walks slowly over to the group of kids. She is soon shaking hands, and striking up a conversation with a young, tired-looking black girl of about eighteen or nineteen.

I stand up, stretch my legs, then head out the bus door and get in line at the men's bathroom. I find myself staring down at the other end of the foyer where Naomi, now with Philip and Jess, are talking to the kids in the lobby. *Wonder what's going on.*

When I walk out of the restroom, I hear Bob announcing over the microphone that we are filled up and ready to roll. Jess and Philip, along with everyone else, are getting back on the bus and I follow suit. But Naomi seems to have other ideas. As I look back out the window, I see she is still in the lobby talking to the same girl and waving her hands about, as if trying to get some point across.

Bob starts the engine and she finally walks back to the bus, but she isn't alone. All twelve of her new friends are in tow behind her. When she stops on the landing above the steps of the bus, they stand outside the bus door. She holds onto the bars on either side of her for support as she speaks.

"May I have everybody's attention, please." Her voice is loud, almost commanding. "These kids behind me are stranded here. They worked for the State Job Corps in the Sierra Mountains east of here. When the Job Corps folded, they made their way down here hoping to get a ride down south to Los Angeles where they live. The problem is that after hanging around here for a couple of days, they don't have enough money for bus tickets, and besides that – the buses are way behind schedule. It could be days before they get a bus going south. I propose we let them ride with us, since we're all going to the same place and we have plenty of room." Naomi catches her breath and then asks, "What do you guys think?"

There is a momentary silence on the bus. No one seems to know what to say. *Share my space? I won't be able to stretch out. But so what? Of course,* I tell myself, *we'll take them. We can't leave them here. It will be fun meeting new people from outside our community.*

To my surprise I hear myself saying in my most confident voice, "Sure, let's take them aboard. It's the least we can do." There is another brief pause.

Then Philip stands up. "I second the idea."

That seems to spark everyone into action, and it's immediately agreed that we'll be pleased to have Naomi's new friends ride with us. Naomi smiles, turns and beckons them to come aboard. The group files on the bus behind Naomi and starts filling up the empty seats.

"Is it all right if I sit here? Is this seat taken?" a husky but feminine voice asks.

I look up in surprise and find myself staring into the round, smiling face of a girl with long, black, braided hair, dark intense eyes, and long earrings that look like wind chimes dangling from her ears. "No, it's not taken," I stammer. "Sure, sit down. Let me help you with your bag." I stand up, reach over the empty seat, and practically pull her old canvas bag out of her hand. She looks at me with a quizzical grin on her face but doesn't say a word. Fortunately, there doesn't seem like there is much in the bag as I try to stuff it into the already full baggage rack over our heads.

"Hi, my name is Jason," I say as I sit back down.

"Hi, back. My name is Holly, and thanks for the help with my bag." And with that she plops into the seat next to me, still wearing her questioning smile.

"Sure, no problem. You from Los Angeles? Is that where you're going?"

"More or less. I live, or should say my parents live, in Pacoima, a suburb of L.A., and that's where I am going at least for the moment. Time to run home to my mama for a while," she says as she reclines her seat back to match mine.

At a loss of words, I glance over at her. She gives me a quick smile back. But the connection seems to be broken and we find ourselves sitting staring straight ahead in silence as our bus pulls out of the depot and heads south on Highway 5. I figure Holly must be about my own age. She is dressed in a faded, wrinkled, red and white plaid shirt, ripped blue jeans, and a dirty pair of white sneakers. She looks tired. I bet she wants to sleep.

"Jason, are you feeling funny, me sitting next to you? I could move over a seat and give you some room... if you're feeling a little shy about having a black girl you don't even know sitting right next to you."

"Oh, I'm fine," I blurt. "I'm not shy, and I'm used to being around girls of all different colors." *Wow! I wonder what brought that on.*

"Hmm. So you have lots of girlfriends, Jason?" she says, raising her eyebrows and looking me right in the eye. "You must be pretty popular back home. So, where are you from?"

"Oh, I'm from Oregon, and I don't have lots of girl-friends," I stammer, trying to gain my composure and figure out where *she* is coming from. "In fact, I don't have any at all, I mean not the romantic type. What I am trying to say is that where I live, boys and girls are raised together and treated equally. We celebrate our differences, but emphasize the fact that we're all basically the same. So it doesn't bother me sitting next to you because you're a girl. I'm used to girls," I add, trying to convince myself as much as her.

"So," Holly says with a grin now stretching from ear to ear, "you guys all sleep together? I mean, in the same room? Or is this one of those free love communes I've read about? Sounds kind of exciting, Jason."

I feel sweat dripping from my armpits, and my shirt is starting to stick to my back. Using my sleeve to wipe my forehead, I end up almost stuttering. "N..no, Holly, you have it all wrong. That's not the way it is at all. I mean, we don't have rules regarding sex. It's strictly an individual thing. We just think people should act responsibly." I try to get the conversation on less personal ground. "Our community decided to have comprehensive sex education taught in our primary schools. By the age of nine or ten we have a good idea what is going on with our bodies and what sex is about. We're encouraged to feel good and natural about our bodies, and never to judge people on theirs."

"It sounds like you guys learn everything in books," Holly interrupts, still wearing her quizzical grin. "Don't you personally ever interact with the girls in your community?"

"Of course, we do," I counter, feeling my adrenaline rising. "As long as I can remember I've always had close female friends. We swim in our pool, tubs, and ponds together without even wearing bathing suits or being embarrassed. I've spent half my life interacting with girls," I boldly announce while wiping my forehead again with my shirt.

"Here, Jason. Here, you can borrow my bandanna." Holly pulls a black bandanna out of her jeans pocket. "Hey, how about sex, Jason? You still a virgin?"

"Uh, well," I stutter, using Holly's bandanna to try and nonchalantly cover my eyes as I wipe my face. *Wow, this girl is sure in my face.* But I've been taught to be open and honest. "I guess I am. I mean, it's like I have so many  friends and so much to do I just haven't had the time to get that involved with one person yet. I feel that I get so much love from everyone in the community, that it just hasn't been necessary. But I admit..." (I hand her back her bandanna.) "...there have been times lately when I think about girls and sex a lot more than I used to."

"Well, I've got to give you credit Jason," says Holly as her eyes start to show a wetness around the corners and her voice takes on more of a high pitch. "I've never heard a boy over 11 even admit he was a virgin before. I think it's pretty cool that you can do that. None of the boys I know would ever have the nerve. They're all too macho. I wish I had known more boys like you when I was growing up."

"How about you?" I quickly ask, seizing the chance to change the subject and the mood.

"You mean am *I* a virgin?"

"No, I mean what have you been doing with your life? Where do you go to school?"

Holly looks me straight in the eye, never cracking a smile, and says in a resigned voice, "Well, Jason, it's like this. I quit junior high when I was thirteen. I've pretty much been homeless ever since. I've been a part-time prostitute for several years now. I do very well when I am in the big city, but just not enough wealthy guys in these smaller towns. I guess I should warn you that I shot two white dudes in a gang fight three years ago, and I stabbed one black bitch that tried to rape me while I was in prison. I spent a year in Folsom Prison before they sent me to the Job Corps to try and rehabilitate me, but as you can see it hasn't worked too well. My motto is: I play without a net. So that in a nutshell is what I've been doing with my life." She continues looking directly at me, not even moving an eyelid.

I shake my head up and down, but my mouth doesn't open and words won't appear. Finally, I turn away, feeling more awkward than before. I wish I could borrow her bandanna again. I hear myself finally mutter, "You certainly live an interesting life, Holly. You certainly do. Makes mine seem awfully tame," I sputter as I pretend to see something out the window that has gotten my attention.

Holly's smile returns and she starts laughing so loud that everyone in the bus seems to look over at us. Her white teeth shine bright as she continues to laugh. "White Boy," she says in a rather patronizing voice and her face looking softer, "you sure are gullible."

*What's up?* I think, beginning to feel like I am missing part of this picture.

"I'm sorry," she says with a smile, her hand on my shoulder, "but you white folks would believe just about anything about us black people."

"Oh," is all I can say as I turn back to face Holly and laugh nervously. But soon we're both laughing uncontrollably, everyone on the bus staring at us and wondering what's going on. Philip smiles and puts his palms up, as if questioning. I smile back and put my palms up in response.

"Well Jason, my reality is that I graduated from high school last year and am supposed to be in college right now, much like you. But because of the state of both the country and my own personal finances, I can't afford college. Unlike you white honkeys, us black people don't have our own personal schools. So I took my black ass... uh... *butt* out and joined the Job Corps. The rest is history."

Her fingertips briefly touch my face and she says, "You know, Jason, you certainly do have lily-white skin. I like your name, okay? But I think I'm gonna call you White Boy. Kind of a nickname." She turns sideways in her seat, hugging her knees as she faces me. "Besides, I can tell just by the way you dress and the way you talk, you need some excitement in your life. Somehow, with a nickname like White Boy, I think you're gonna get lots of attention."

Not slowing down to ask me what I think, she just keeps right on talking. "So, White Boy, why're you guys heading south? Everybody else is trying to get out, and you're going in! Ya know, Disneyland is only open on weekends now. Just not enough tourists to stay open all week. So what are you guys gonna do down there?"

*Good question* I say to myself, one I'm still not sure I have a complete answer to. Everything's happened so fast. First, President Bradshaw, after two years of brutal attacks by fellow politicians and the media, resigned suddenly. The government actually collapsed for three days when all the lawmakers fled Washington during the riots that ensued. Meanwhile, Vice President Deborah Mandell was trapped in the out of season hurricane that devastated much of South Carolina at the same time. After her rescue from her home in Charleston, she took over – our first woman president. She immediately declared a national state of emergency and martial law in eleven cities including L.A., San Francisco and, of course, Washington, D.C. Regular Army troops, along with police and National Guards from Virginia, had to retake our capitol street by street in fierce fighting that left several hundred dead and wounded.

President Mandell said the nation was in a life-or-death struggle to survive. She believes we need a new direction on both personal and national levels.

Then she came to our community and asked for help, having studied and stayed in one of our communities for six months, five years ago. She said she thinks we have found a rational, sane way to live. She wants us to help form a new national Peace Corps, to go into large cities and work with the people. And we're to come up with a workable model of a new community right smack in the middle of one of our country's most devastated areas.

It's amazing to me! Here I am on a bus heading for L.A. when only three weeks ago leaving Higher Ground had not even crossed my mind. Now I am part of a mission that most people would think almost impossible, to say the least. How can I explain all of this to Holly?

"Holly," I hear myself saying cautiously. "We're heading for L.A. as part of the new Peace Corps the President has authorized. We're going down there to help rebuild the city, or at least the part that's been burned down, right in the middle of what I believe is called Watts. We're going to build houses out of tires. We'll build park areas instead of streets, free medical clinics, community centers, and basically a whole new community. We're even going to help revamp the schools and start teaching the kids what's really important, like love and self-esteem instead of just subjects like algebra and French."

We are both quiet for a moment. "That's it. That's what we're going to do, in a nutshell."

Holly doesn't say a word for several seconds, just looks me straight in the eye with a blank look on her face. Finally, she shakes her head slowly back and forth, her braids and earrings brushing across the side of her face. "White Boy, that's real nice, great idea." She shakes her head some more, gives me a solemn quizzical look, then turns around and says, "I gotta get some sleep. G'night."

I barely get a chance to say my own goodnight when she lies back against her seat, closes her eyes, and looks like she's pretending to sleep.

*Oh my God! I shouldn't have opened my big mouth* I haven't been this embarrassed many times in my nineteen years, but I am now. *She thinks we're a bunch of lunatics.* I don't know where I'm going or what I'm doing. I sit quietly, embarrassed, pretending to be asleep and wishing this night would quickly end.

Then slowly, Holly opens her eyes and turns to me. "Um, White Boy, I know you're not sleeping, and I don't want to sound mean, but ya do know you're crazy? You know, you sound like some Jesus freak or something. All this love-your-neighbor shit. You're going to the toughest, meanest part of one of the roughest cities in the world and save those folks, right? What you got? A magic wand or something? They're going to eat you alive, spit out what's left, and stomp on it 'til it's dust. Man, you guys seem nice and everything, but you're nuts! You do know that, don't you?"

She shakes her head again, turns back square in the seat, folds her arms, and again closes her eyes. I do the same, not knowing how to respond, hoping for a miracle that will make

Holly magically disappear, sparing me further embarrassment.

Holly can't pretend sleeping for long though. Soon she turns back towards me and, with a patronizing smile, pokes me in the arm and asks, "White Boy, tell me about your parents, where you live, where you go to school, all that kind of stuff. All that real stuff we can put in your obituary."

"Well," I answer, trying to gain my composure, "I don't know much about my mom. She left when I was pretty young, about two or three, before we lived in the community. I haven't hardly seen her since. Last time I heard from her she was living in Brentwood, California. Married to some type of lawyer. Maybe I'll look her up while I am down there. Anyway, my dad raised me – my dad and the community. You see, in our community everyone gets involved in raising the children, not just the parents. I feel like I have a hundred uncles and aunts. I lived with my dad until I was fifteen, and then I moved into one of the dormitories to get ready for college."

"College at fifteen? What are you, a genius or something?"

"No, surely not," I laugh and think to myself, *That'll be the day.* "Most everyone graduates from school at fifteen or sixteen in our community. We don't spend a lot of time learning what most public schools think is important. We learn to read and write by the time we're ten. From then on we spend most school time talking and studying about life, spirituality and self-esteem, what makes us tick, how we can get along, why we love, why we hate and fight wars, that kind of stuff. By the time we're fifteen, we have a pretty good grip on what's going on. We're ready for college."

"Give me a break Jason. What college is going to take a bunch of fifteen-year-olds who think they know it all? Certainly no college I know of."

"We have our own colleges," I add, glad to be talking on a subject I know more about, one not quite so personal. "We have 52 communities in our co-op. Our co-op is a loose-knit group of communities with some of the same ideals. Twelve of them have colleges. That's where most of us go. I go to school right in my own community. I was supposed to finish college this year, but it now looks like that's on hold for a while."

Holly interrupts me, her eyes held wide and her mouth exaggerating the words as she talks. "White Boy, you might be on hold for a long, long time if you're going to L.A. But if you believe in reincarnation, which I suppose you do, maybe next lifetime you'll finish. So what are you majoring in? Helping I and II?"

"Well," I continue with a laugh, "in community school, which we're in 'til we're fifteen or sixteen, we learn the basics of living and reading and writing. In college we prepare for our vocation. I'm studying solar engineering. Solar power is the main source of energy in most of our communities. That's what I hope I'll be doing in L.A., helping to build solar power plants and green houses."

"Sounds interesting; just a little idealistic, but interesting. If nothing else, we get plenty of sunshine in L.A., and power has gotten so expensive. At my parents' home we're lucky to keep a roof over our heads." Then she adds sarcastically, "We don't have money for frills like electricity, transportation, and things like that."

We're talking in my field of interest now, and I can feel my voice rising as I get more excited. "That's the whole idea! To build you houses that are energy efficient and produce their own really cheap, clean energy."

"Are these the houses out of the tires you mentioned earlier? I don't believe you guys really live in houses made out of tires."

"Sure, some of us do. Some are straw houses, and lots are  made out of recycled polyurethane called stress skin panels. My dad's house is a tire, or what we call an *earthship.* That's what some of them are called... because they're almost totally self-sufficient. Tire houses have been around since the 1980's. Look, let me explain. Tires are the inside. You don't see the tires from the outside or the inside; they're like the framing in an old house. All you see is adobe. The tires are interlocked, filled with sand and packed down, and can withstand even the strong earthquakes you guys have in Southern California. "

Now Holly looks at me intently, squirms in her seat and gets more comfortable. So I continue. "Heaven knows, we have plenty of tires to get rid of. In fact, there're supposed to be two million of them waiting for us in Watts right now. Unskilled labor can build the tire houses; you can do it with one foreman and lots of hands. It's a lot of hard work, but with scarcity of lumber and prices what they are, the tire houses are way cheaper to build; and there are no energy costs after they're done. They're perfect for L.A. With their adobe finish, they have a Spanish look and will fit in from what I hear of your architectural style."

"Well, unfortunately, we have lots of unskilled labor in L.A., especially in Watts," Holly sighs. "Since Watts is burned to the ground, we need houses; but how you'll ever get people to work together to build them is beyond me. It will take more than a miracle. It will take the Army, Marines, plus the National Guard. And you'd better hope God is on your side because you're going to need him or her, or both, or actually anybody you can get!"

We both laugh half-heartedly, but at least I'm glad I can still laugh. After hearing Holly talk, I have a sinking feeling I might be doing a lot less laughing in the coming months. There is a pause in our conversation; I think we're both out of breath.

Naomi gets up from her seat in the front of the bus and walks towards us. "How're you guys doing?" she asks, standing in the aisle, steadying herself by leaning against the outside seat. "Looks like you're hitting it off. At least you're talking and laughing."

"Hi, Naomi," I answer. "I think you've already met Holly. In fact, you two seemed responsible for getting the whole group on the bus. Good work. You've always been an instigator, or maybe *catalyst* is a better word."

"Thanks, Jason," says Naomi with a smirk. "You've always had a way with words, but I do like the latter definition better."

"Want to sit down?" I reach around Holly and move my jacket out of the way.

"Come on; there's room for one more," Holly says. "Besides, Jason here likes girls; the more the merrier for him."

"Sure," Naomi says with a laugh as she sits down in the outside seat. "You've known each other for two hours. You've got to be tired of each other by now. We're just outside Stockton. Bob says another six hours and we're in L.A. Kind of scary, but exciting too, huh?"

"More scary than exciting," I reply. "At least according to Holly. She thinks we're some kind of Jesus-freaks. She thinks we're going to end up in a lot of trouble in L.A. – big-time trouble. Naomi, maybe you could explain to Holly what we're about and what we're doing. I'm not sure I am getting through to her." I put my hands behind my neck, lean back in my seat, and figure this is a good time to rest my jaws.

"Well, we're not Jesus-freaks. In fact, some of us are Buddhists, Hindus and agnostics. We're a non-denominational, non-sectarian community. We practice basic Christian values, and most of us certainly love who Jesus was, but we're not of any one religion. There is no guru or anything

45

like that. We've just gotten down to the basics of learning and practicing to love thy neighbor as you would yourself. Many of us get a lot of our lifestyle ideas from *A Course in Miracles*, which is a spiritual, non-dogmatic course in simply learning to replace fear with love."

"I've heard of that," Holly interrupts excitedly. "There's no church or anything, right? It just teaches you how to find God through yourself, by letting go of your ego and practicing replacing fear with love."

"That's right. You've got it," Naomi says.

"Yeah, I've talked with some of my friends about the course. I have a girlfriend who's studying it, and I've seen Marianne Williamson on the *Oprah* show. I've got to admit, I like the ideas in it, though it may not seem so practical in Watts. So, the *Course in Miracles* is what you guys try to live by? At least I can relate to that."

"Yes, that's really what our community is about. We've learned through the *Course* that it is our choice to create the reality of love, forgiveness and joy instead of fear, drama, anger and unhappiness; we try to support one another in living it all the time. The support is the secret. Plus we each have our own individual practice that reinforces our life. It's a kick, Holly; it really is. I know it sounds idealistic, but it really does work. It's a lot more fun being loving and happy than being angry and sad, and we really do have a good time most of the time."

"Naomi," I laugh, "I think it's *you* who's always had a way with words. Basically though, you said it all. We're just trying to live a more practical, happy, fulfilling life. That's all. We work at it all the time. Sometimes it's really hard, but most of the time it pays off big time."

"Oh, Jason," says Naomi as she turns towards me, "you always say everything in such a serious way." She gives me a mock scolding look and then pats me on my back, like one would a lost puppy.

"You guys make this place you live in sound awful nice," Holly says with a sigh. "Maybe if you live through L.A., I'll go back with you and visit your community in Oregon. I'd like to take a look for myself. I am not sure I believe half of what you're saying, but you two seem more sincere than the average zealots. I take back what I said about you guys being Jesus-freaks. You're just a little strange for this world, that's all."

This time we all laugh together, and I feel a connectedness growing. Holly and Naomi turn toward each other and slap each other's hands, give the "hi" sign. Then Holly asks, "How do you guys govern this Utopia anyway? Our city government is so corrupt in L.A. Everyone knows that. Many of our politicians are either corrupt, inept, or on a total ego trip. Even the good ones can't get through the bureaucracy to get anything done. So, what do you guys do differently?"

"Well," Naomi says, always ready to jump in, "we don't have any professional politicians, or much of a bureaucracy. I was a City Councilwoman for the last two years and it was fun. Our communities are run by a City Council just like your cities, but our council members are picked out of a hat. They don't run for election. That way the ego doesn't get so involved. We have ten council people. All are appointed for two years, five each year. Everyone over eighteen serves eventually, unless they feel they really don't want to do it. We have a professional community manager and a small staff like your city. These people help keep the continuity flowing when we get new council members. We try to do everything by consensus, but the bigger decisions are made by referendums. Every six months there is a referendum on the important issues in the community. Then it's up to the council and City Manager to carry out the decisions."

Naomi turns in her seat towards Holly, puts her legs underneath her, and continues, obviously excited about what she's saying. "Almost everything else is done by the citizens. We all put in twenty hours a month of labor. And not for pay. That's where we get much of our work force. It works pretty well. We really work at giving up our personal agendas when it comes to community matters and because we try to practice honest communication, we have a very high trust level. It doesn't always please everyone, but we all know we've been heard and have been part of the decision. Our system glorifies no one. If a person happens to be a temporary leader, we know he is just doing his part and next time it will be somebody else's turn. I'd guess you'd say we have no heroes. We really don't believe in them."

"Well, white folks, you guys make it sound good, that's for sure. Maybe too good to be true. I've got one more question, then I really do have to get some sleep. We're supposed to hit L.A. at first light, and I want to be awake to see your pretty white faces when you see the city, or what's left of it. My question is – how do you guys make a living? How does your community get money? Who owns it? I know you guys are not on welfare, because they ran out of money months ago. Do you have real jobs when you're not out saving the world?"

"I'll take this one," I say to Naomi before she has a chance to get started. "It's the most complicated part of our community, but I'll try to make it simple. All of our members own shares in our community, since it is a for profit corporation. The land is a land trust, and we own it forever; it was paid off years ago. All of our buildings are built by our own labor crews and our own money. We scrounge for materials – like our tires, for example. But really, our houses – in fact all of our buildings – are very nice. Our whole community is designed to adapt to the environment instead of making our environment adapt to us. Everything seems to fit together. We live simply, but very comfortably. We don't have any big ostentatious houses or fancy cars, and I doubt that you'll see any of us wearing fur coats."

"Don't make it sound so boring," Naomi scolds. "We have tons of fun. Since most of us work only six hours a day, we have all kinds of time to do art, crafts, sports, hiking, plays, classes, music, meditations, groups – all sorts of playing. It's free, and the facilities are all within walking distance of one another. Childcare is available right up until bedtime. This gives everyone a chance to participate. We try to make sure no one gets left out, unless that's what he or she desires. Sometimes we all need to be alone, just to meditate or contemplate, so we also try to give everyone his own space."

Naomi continues, waving her hands as she talks. "While I'm on the subject of childcare, it's considered the most important job at Higher Ground. Our most loving and honored people work in our childcare centers. They get the same rate of return as doctors or anyone else in a helping profession. Our children are our first priority, yet not at the expense of the mother or father. Everyone pitches in. You should see all the grandmas and grandpas volunteering at our childcare centers. It's really a warm, friendly atmosphere. Our childcare centers are the closest thing to heaven on earth," Naomi says in her most earnest voice.

"But, guys, you still haven't explained how you pay for all this great stuff. Somebody's got to pay for it all."

"Naomi got off track there a little," I add, "though everything she said is true. We have 61 separate businesses at Higher Ground, all of them being what we call sustainable. That means that they produce only things that we as a group feel are positive contributions to people's lives. The people who work in them own them. There are no stockholders or individual owners, unless it's a family or one-person business. All the rest are co-ops. Since everyone in reality is working for himself, people work hard. All our businesses are divided into teams that work together in mastermind groups. We usually work six-hour shifts with only a small break. We estimate we get one-third more done than most other eight-hour a day employees. We do have managers that oversee operations, but the employees elect them. The amazing part is we get no pay per se. That means the business has no payroll – which is by far the biggest expense. Our businesses pay no rent because the community owns the buildings. Utilities are not a big expense since we produce our own electricity at very little cost. Also, everything is made with extra care to quality and detail. Pride in our workmanship is a big thing, so our products are always in demand. Our prices are usually less than those of businesses outside our community because our expenses are so small. Our publishing company is a good example of such a business."

"But how?" Holly stifles a yawn but I can tell it's from weariness, not boredom. "How can you get people to work for free? It sounds a lot like socialism."

"It's pretty simple," I tell her. "People don't really work for free. Our businesses make an excellent net profit because their cost of doing business is so low. The profit is split 50/50. The community gets half, and the employees get half. The community's half goes toward paying the expenses of running the community, such as housing, water, sewer, maintenance, electricity, that sort of thing. The community also provides for most of the primary needs of the employee – like medical services, much of our food, childcare, and utilities. Because it's so inexpensive to live at Higher Ground, just one flat fee of $500 per month per family includes everything. The community member is often able to save much of his money, though he or she doesn't need it while living in our community. We do much of our community interacting using the barter system.

"You have to remember that people are totally free to come and go, sell their stock, and take their savings and leave. A few do move, some to other communities that have different structures than ours, but not too many – probably less than one percent a year."

Now it's Holly who's waving her hands. "But how did you get people to do this? What motivated them? People are naturally greedy, selfish, and competitive."

"I can remember when I was little, eight or nine years old," I tell her. "We were having a big community meeting about our schools. After a while the whole thing seemed to get out of hand; everyone seemed to be arguing and it got really heated. Some people stomped out of the room and never came back. I mean never. I was scared, actually devastated.

"Some of us younger ones thought the community was falling apart. Then the rest of the group closed ranks and we became even closer. That seemed to be a turning point. After that, they always worked at making every meeting a win/win situation. But if some people chose to go their own way, that was okay. That just became part of the process.

"It comes down to everyone's willingness to give up the illusion of personal freedom. Personal freedom in your culture means it's your choice to be you against the world. It's all for one and one for all in our culture. We don't waste a lot of energy on competition, ego trips, or the negative things that sap the energy out of a community and its people. In our community there isn't a value put on how much money someone makes or has accumulated, or how big a house they live in. Without a big discrepancy in wages, people tend to find their value through who they are as a person, and in doing what they get value out of.

"This is what concerns me about L.A. The people there are still battling against one another and, as far as I know, haven't made these commitments. So how do we motivate them to reprogram themselves? That's the real challenge, isn't it, Holly?"

I hear no reply from Holly or Naomi except their heavy breathing. Their eyes are closed. *They are both asleep!* It is past midnight and I too can feel sleep close at hand. I'd been rambling, but I feel Holly and Naomi would have agreed with my last statement... had they been awake. I close my eyes and stretch my legs, knowing when I awaken we will be in L.A.

When two cultures collide
is the time when
true suffering exists.

Albert Camus

# Chapter 5

I am not sure if it's Naomi and Holly's whispering that awakens me, or if it is the first crack of light peeking through the window. I am slumped down in my seat, and try to get the energy to sit up when I hear, "Hey, White Boy, you're here. Look out your window. We're entering L.A."

I sit up with a start and try to wipe the sleep out of my eyes. I give a quick "good morning" to both Holly and Naomi, but my eyes immediately go to my window to get my first glimpse of the San Fernando Valley at sunrise. We are on a freeway perched at least fifty feet above the valley floor. The sun's just peeking through a brown haze from the East, but I can see for many miles in both directions. Holly leans over and quietly tells me that the San Fernando Valley is a suburb of L.A. and that we're still about fifteen miles from downtown.

The city looks somewhat like I had pictured it – houses and apartments of all shapes and sizes as far as I can see. Large asphalt streets divide the houses into little squares that seem to go on forever. There are hundreds of cars, trucks and vans, but few are moving at this hour. I glance at my watch; it's only 5:36, but I am wide-awake now.

As we travel down the freeway, everything looks very, very dry. Not one green lawn. Only deep-rooted shrubs and trees have managed to survive the last three years of drought; they are the only living green to be seen.

"See all those swimming pools?" Holly nonchalantly points out the window to backyard after backyard of empty pools. "Not one of them has water in it. Hasn't been enough water for lawns or pools but twice in the last six years. Four years ago we got 26 inches of rain and major flooding. The last three years we've averaged less than three inches a year. Something to do with the greenhouse effect. The weather is getting crazier every year. We're on water rationing: six hours on, six hours off. The fires started in a part of town where the water was shut down, and no one could get through the bureaucracy to get it turned on 'til it was too late. That's why so much of the city burned. There was simply no water to use to fight the fires."

When I feel Bob slowing the bus down I see a freeway exit sign that says *Victory Blvd.* At first I think we're going to pull off the freeway. *Is this Watts?* Looking up, I see Bob staring intently off to his left as the bus almost comes to a complete stop. It's as if all of a sudden the city ends. On one side of Victory Blvd. houses and businesses are lined up. On the other side are blocks and blocks of nothing but black rubble. I look over at Holly to ask what is going on, but I keep my mouth closed when I see her staring around me, her dark eyes glaring coldly out the window at the devastation.

She slowly opens her mouth and, talking to no one in particular, says, "People got tired of just the black part of town being burned down. So after a while they came over here where white and brown people lived... and burned it. You can see back there at Victory Blvd." She points at the direction we just came from. "That's where the fire started. Then it went south from there to the base of the Hollywood Hills. It all burned. A couple thousand houses and over 300 businesses were lost in this fire." Her voice is a low monotone, kind of aloof. "It was a big one, but nothing like you'll see on the other side of Hollywood Hills." That said, she crosses her arms, her face goes blank, and she slowly slides down into her seat.

Naomi and I look around Holly and our eyes connect as we stare at each other in silence. You can't hear a word being spoken by any of our members. Naomi leans forward and goes back to staring out the window. I look back at Philip, but his face is glued to the window. I think he's in shock, looking at the scars of the fires.

Holly's companions, scattered around the bus, don't seem to be so in awe of the fire damage. In fact, I hear several of them making a game out of reciting the names of each street that has burned.

Freddie Dole, a tall slender black kid who looks maybe nineteen, gruffly makes a loud pronouncement. "I think the L.A. Fire Department should have let the whole Valley burn and get rid of, once and for all, the rich honkeys and Asians who own and run the city."

Naomi, her face pale and drawn, turns from the window and says to Holly, "I've read about the fires, but I've never quite understood who started them and why. Was it black people who were angry, or angry white people who burned these buildings and houses? It doesn't make any sense to me. It's so destructive. I don't understand it."

"Well, let me tell you a few things." It's Luella from across the aisle, one of the twelve people we picked up in Sacramento. She's a large girl with intense black eyes, and she's been very quiet until now. In fact, this is the first time I've heard her speak. It's obvious from the high pitch in her voice that she's very agitated. When she speaks, everyone turns around to listen.

"It wasn't just us black people who did the burning. It was whites, browns, and yellow people too. It used to be just black people who rioted and burned; we were the ones without jobs, decent housing, and enough food. But ever since the Stock Market broke in '07, you white people started going without too. And you don't like it at all! These fires here in the Valley were started by angry white and brown people, not just black people," she exclaims, waving her arms around. "Everyone wants better pay, better jobs and living conditions, and just plain better lives." With that, like someone turned a switch, she folds her arms across her chest, sits down in her seat and stares out her window. I guess she's said what she wanted to say,

I don't know what to think. The Valley is what I imagine a war zone would look like. I try to focus my mind on other things around me besides the destruction we've just witnessed and the intensity of the feelings. I glance at Naomi, but she's closed her eyes, put her hands in her lap, and seems to have gone into a meditation.

Our bus climbs the freeway into what a large green sign says is the Hollywood Hills. Traffic is light, and I'm at least glad to see most of the cars that are running are electric, not gas.

Hoping to change the subject and lighten things up, I mention this to Holly. She sits up in her seat and quietly points out that L.A. has tried banning all but electric cars to help fight pollution, but people still drive their gas guzzlers when gas is available. "But gas is scarce," she says in an emotionless tone, "and at $6.00 a gallon, not many can afford it. Most people, if they don't have an electric car, have adapted by using the mass transit system, which they once avoided like the plague... until they had no other choice."

"I guess most people don't change until there's a crisis," I say.

"Guess not," Holly says flatly as she turns forward in her seat. I do the same.

"Well, folks," Bob says quietly into the microphone, "this is L.A., as I am sure you figured out. In about ten minutes we'll be on the outskirts of Compton and Watts, where you'll be staying. There should be officials from the city and federal governments there to meet us. They'll brief you on what's going on. I'll be heading back up north in this old rented jalopy to pick up some more members from a community near Crescent City, California. I just want to wish everyone good luck, and may peace go with you."

I knew we rented this old gas-guzzler because our electrical vans were too small, but I hadn't thought about Bob and the bus not being around if we needed to get out. The churning feeling in the pit of my stomach is returning. *What I am doing here? Why have I left the security of my community?* Holly's aloofness doesn't help either. It's like her mind has left and her body is still sitting next to me, going through the motions. *Is everyone else on the bus as nervous as I am? Here I am, about to enter into the first really big adventure of my life, and I'm wondering what I've gotten into.*

The sky is still pinkish gray in the east as our bus comes out of the Hollywood Hills into the haze of downtown L.A. It's 6:05 a.m. on Saturday, April 7, 2012. L.A. still exists – despite earthquakes, drought, floods, riots, pollution, violence, and now fires. Yes, the city is still standing – or more correctly, the larger part of it is.

We drive past skyscrapers of downtown, and as we travel southwest, the city looks more dilapidated all the time. Boarded up houses and businesses are visible on both sides of the freeway. Trash seems to have accumulated everywhere I look. In a town where reportedly tens of thousands of people are sleeping in tents, with no place to go after the last fires, I wonder why I see so many vacant houses.

"You see all these empty houses, White Boy?" Holly says wistfully as we both stare out our window. "Most of them are condemned. And when displaced people try to move in, the city officials have them evicted. This is one of the issues that started the rioting... that led to the fires... that burned down so much of our city." Holly crosses her arms, looks straight ahead, and is again silent.

Her friends have also gotten strangely quiet in the last few minutes as we near what was once their hometown. They no longer display the exuberance they felt when pointing out the burnt streets in the San Fernando Valley. An eerie tension passes through the passengers on the bus as we travel the last several miles to our destination.

"Look over there!" says Holly as she breaks her silence and points out the window. "That's where the fires started here in Watts. They say it goes for eleven miles west and about nine miles south. Everything is burned in that whole area. Nothing is left, not one single house."

We all strain to see out the windows as older Spanish-style stucco houses and buildings give way to the black rubble that was once the Watts-Compton area of L.A. As far as the eye can see, there is nothing but the black burned-out shell, once a community where Holly and the others grew up. They say it was a very rough community, but it had been their home – the only one most of them had ever known.

Their silence is deafening. The fires were many months ago and, from what I understand, these kids left knowing what their city looked like. But coming back and seeing it again seems to be shocking them right down to their cores.

"Well, White Boy, this is it," Holly says in her subdued voice. "This is where I grew up. My parents live in Pacoima, north of here, now, but this was my home until I was 16. That's when my dad decided we had to get out of Watts, and the violence and poverty that went with it. All the rest of the kids had their homes burned in the fires. Their families are scattered about. Some live in the tent cities. Who knows where the others are."

I look out my window at the mass destruction and am at a loss for words. I realize for the first time that these kids are coming back to nothing. Their homes and community burned to the ground. Their families are scattered. They, like us, are feeling like aliens in a foreign land. I ask myself if any of us really belong here.

Bob puts on the right blinker of the bus, and we slow to a crawl as we exit the freeway and roll down a long, empty off-ramp. We are immediately stopped at the bottom of the ramp. Four camouflaged-clad soldiers with some type of large rifle on their hips are sitting on the top of a large armored vehicle blocking our way. One of them – a stocky, stern-looking man with a crew cut and four white stripes on his camouflage uniform shoulder – climbs down a ladder and walks our way.

"Hello," the soldier says as he walks up the stairs of our bus and greets Bob in a deep southern drawl. "Sergeant Phillips, Fourth Cavalry. Welcome to Watts. I'll need to see your passes and identification cards. This is a closed zone, under martial law by the order of the President. Everyone entering must have passes and identification before we can let your bus off the ramp." His eyes rest briefly on Holly, then on several of the other black kids. He turns to Bob who, with a blank expression, takes out a manila envelope and hands the soldier a packet of papers.

The sergeant thumbs through the papers, stopping at one in particular. "Hmmm... This one is signed by the President herself!" He looks back up at Bob. "You all must be pretty important to have the *President* sign your orders. Is everybody on the bus part of your group?"

"Sure are. They've all come down from up north to help you rebuild this place." Bob says as he spreads his arms in an arc across the windshield of the bus.

"Well, we certainly can use all the help we can get," says the sergeant as he looks slowly around the bus one last time. "But I am not sure what help you folks can be. It's a total disaster." He points out the front window at some large machines moving about. "The Army Corps of Engineers is out there with its bulldozers, and all they can do is smash and pile up the rubble. We've got nothing to build new housing with, and now the county trucks are hauling in old tires from all the dumps in the city. They're just dumping them out wherever we clean up. Doesn't make any sense to anyone. Personally, I think the whole world has gone mad. Anyway, you people can go ahead. Everything looks in order. Pull into that large cleared parking area." He points straight ahead. "Good luck. We'll try to give you protection while you're here but, as I am sure you've been told, we can't guarantee anything – anything at all."

The sergeant smartly turns and, without looking back, steps off the bus and walks back to his armored car. The driver starts the motor, and the soldiers move their vehicle just far enough out of the way for us to pass.

Bob releases the brake and starts the engine. As we pass the armored vehicle, a soldier with a camouflaged hard hat and no smile keeps his machine gun pointed directly at us. We pull down to a large pot-holed parking lot, devoid of any civilian cars or buses. Only a handful of Army and police vehicles occupy the lot.

As the bus comes to a stop, Naomi walks to the front and turns to face us. "Sounds like we got some new recruits," she says through a tight grin. "You guys used to live here but now have nowhere to go. And it sounds like nothing to do. We're here to help rebuild your community. The Army thinks you're all with us, and so do I. We've been promised three meals a day, a tent to sleep in, and some type of protection. Sounds like that's more than you'll get on your own. I think I speak for all of us in saying we would like you to join us."

There's a murmur of "definitely" and "sign them up" that passes through the bus as we all give our verbal agreement to what Naomi said.

The bus becomes very quiet again. Finally, Holly stands up and looks around. "I don't know about the rest of you guys, but count me in. My mom always said I was a masochist. This seems a good time as any to prove her right. I do have a place to call home, but no job and no money for school. Besides, I kind of like these people." She gives me a wink. "Even if I do think they're a little weird and naive."

Holly continues standing, and then one by one Luella, Bobbie, Bennie and the other members of her group stand up and count themselves in. Only one, Freddie Dole, the tall lanky one with the crewcut, bows out. "No. Sorry, but man, there ain't no way this is going to work. This ain't no fairy tale, and Watts ain't no Fairyland. The Army ain't gonna be able to protect you, and man, did you see that dude with that machine gun pointed right at us when we drove by? That's the dude who's supposed to be protecting us. This is crazy. And how you ever going to rebuild a mess like this when no one gives a shit? Sorry. Count me out." Freddie grabs his bag and, with his head down, walks off the bus into the hazy sunshine of L.A.

After a minute of hesitation, the rest of us grab our bags from the racks overhead and quietly head for the door. Holly and Naomi are in front of me and in back of me, and I can see Philip and Melissa already out the door and heading across the lot. Bob stands near his seat and gives everyone a hug before they step down.

"Bye, Bob. Thanks a lot." This is all I can say as I wait above the stairs for my turn to get off the bus. That queasy feeling has again taken up residence in my stomach. I try to act very calm, but Bob can see right through me.

"You be careful, Jason," he chuckles. "You stick with these two girls. You'll be just like the Three Musketeers. You guys are going to get something good done here. I can feel it. Peace be with you."

Bob gives me a big hug and I step off the bus, smiling to myself, even though I am really not sure who the Three Musketeers are. But I like the connotation. It feels good to have Holly on one side and Naomi on the other. The three of us, following behind the rest of our group, walk arm in arm toward several police officers sitting at a table under what looks like an elm tree – the only living green object I see.

As we walk I notice that as far ahead as I can see, everything's been leveled. There's nothing but charred ground with big piles of scattered rubble. Except for the rumble of distant bulldozers, there isn't a sound – not a bird chirping or a dog barking. To our left are hundreds of drab green tents. They're set in long rows, several blocks long. I don't see many people around. It is still early, so I figure most people aren't up yet.

Behind me and to the north I see unburned streets and houses. That's the border... where the fire was contained. From here I can't tell if anybody lives in the houses, but I can see one lone soldier with a rifle strapped to his back, walking back and forth on patrol.

When we approach the police officers at the table in front of us, Holly's arm becomes very stiff in mine. "White Boy, I don't like cops. Even black ones. This part is making me very nervous."

"We've been expecting you," is the greeting our group receives from a large black man sitting at one of the two tables. His nametag identifies him as Lieutenant Spencer of the L.A.P.D. "You're the third bus of community members who have arrived here so far. We've also had two busloads of Habitat for Humanity people come this morning. You wouldn't believe who was on their first bus," he adds, momentarily sounding excited. He answers his own question without giving any of us a chance to reply. "Jimmy Carter! You younger kids wouldn't remember him. He was President almost 30 years ago. He must be around 85 by now, and he's still building houses for poor people. He even looks pretty good. Not much hair left, a lot of wrinkles, but he still smiles a lot. I've got to admit, even if I am a Republican and he's a Democrat, he's a pretty remarkable guy. Nice to have an ex-president here." Lt. Spencer continues nonstop, though now more serious and maybe a little embarrassed for showing so much excitement. "Gives us some credibility to what we're trying to do. Not that I'm exactly sure what that is."

Spencer now turns away to hand another officer our papers. This moves us, in a group, to another black officer who introduces himself as Corporal Marken. Marken assigns us to one of the large green tents we just passed. He says it'll be our home while we are in L.A. "You people be careful about leaving food about in your tents," he adds. "We've got an epidemic of giant kangaroo rats overrunning this place. They have become immune to our poisons, and some of them weigh up to ten pounds. Ferocious little buggers. So watch your step."

We all thank him for his advice, acting very causal about his announcement. But as we take a few steps away, both Holly and Naomi go "Yuck," stick their fingers in their mouths and roll their eyes.

We walk the several hundred yards or so to our new home, Marv stays to talk to the city and county officials. Now that Bob's gone, Marv is our spokesman. The group decided that the morning we left. Marv is the oldest male member with us. He's tall and lanky, has a good head of silver hair, an ever-ready smile, a gleam in his eye, and a good word to say about everybody.

"Hey, White Boy, now that we've made it through the check station without them throwing us black kids in jail, I've got another question for you. I thought you guys don't have any leaders at this commune you live in. So how come this Marv guy is acting like he is in charge back there?"

"Well, we don't really have leaders per se at Higher Ground," I explain as we walk. "What we often do is let one person arise as our spokesman for a given period of time.

That individual merits no particular status, but he or she fulfills his public service and we appreciate the effort. The person receives and disseminates the information the group needs, the group makes decisions on it, then the leader takes action. Sometimes the process is a little cumbersome, but the benefits of group participation are well worth it. Anyway, that's what Marv is doing now; he is our temporary leader."

"Well, I can't believe all this works. I have lots *more* questions, White Boy, but I'll hold them 'til later. Let's check out our accommodations; this doesn't look like a Holiday Inn. Looks more like our *'suites'* at Job Corps, which isn't a very good sign."

Our tents are large. Their sides open up to let a light breeze pass through. They are olive green and faded from use. There are twelve steel bunk beds in each and beside each bed is a large metal stand-up locker that can be used as both a dressing room and closet. Two footlockers are tucked underneath each bunk. Outside are portable outhouses and temporary wash stands. A sitting area in the front of each tent and a pile of metal chairs on the dirt floor pose as a lounge area. We throw our bags under the bunks we choose. Each tent seems to be coed; everyone just wanders into whichever one is handy.

I look around for Philip, but he must have gone into one of the other tents where the rest of our community members are. Holly and Naomi pick the bunks right next to mine. Holly takes the top and Naomi the bottom. I pick the top bunk and the bottom one stays empty, at least for the moment.

"White Boy, we ain't letting you get too far away from us," chides Holly as she sits cross-legged on top of her bunk. "Remember what Bob said? We're supposed to stick to-gether, and us gals are supposed to take care of you. So you mind what we tell you."

"I remember about sticking together, but I don't remember anything about you two taking care of me. I'm a big boy, and we can all take care of one another."

Naomi gives me a knowing smile back. *What's going on here?* I wonder. *I feel like I'm missing part of the picture,* I think as I climb upon my bed and lie back on my pillow. *I'll unpack later.* The mattress is thick but lumpy and has a musty odor. I suppose I'll get used to it.

I listen to Naomi and Holly talk and laugh as they unpack and hang up their clothes. They do not seem to share my nervousness about our adventure. Their mood now seems to be earnest and light-hearted. The heaviness of a couple hours ago seems to have fled.

That's great for them, but I realize I'm just more serious. Friends have always told me that my temperament is like an oak tree: sturdy and resilient, but not too flamboyant or exciting. In our community, most of us believe being negative saps not only the energy of the person being negative, but also steals energy from the people around him. I don't want to take energy from anyone; I want to be a giver. I guess I'll just have to be the contemplative one of this bunch.

We pass the rest of the day visiting, sharing, and doing yoga.

"I guess we'll have to wait until tomorrow to learn the city's plan for us," Marv says as he walks back into the tent several hours later. "It sounds like no one is in charge out there yet, but I am sure they'll figure it out," he adds, looking around the room with what looks like a glued-on smile.

By nightfall, the long bus ride is catching up with me, and I lie back on my bunk. It's getting late, and I don't want to bother getting up for dinner. Officer Jenkins told us that somewhere in the midst of this sea of tents the Army had set up a portable mess hall to feed us. I've been snacking all day on crackers and cheese, so I'm not really hungry.

I feel myself drifting off to sleep when the next thing I hear is, "Jason, wake up." It sounds like Naomi. I try opening my eyes, but they feel heavy and don't want to open. Slowly, I start to focus and remember where I am.

"Come on, Jason, wake up and follow me."

"Oh, hi, Naomi. What's going on?" I manage to literally spit the words out of my cotton-feeling mouth. I sit up in my bed, stretch, then quietly slide down from the top bunk. I grab my pants from my locker and pull them on. I glance up at Holly sprawled across her bunk with one arm drooping off the side and her eyes shut tight. Naomi, already dressed in jeans and t-shirt, beckons me to follow.

The air is still warm even though it must be past midnight. There's almost a full moon peeking through the end of our tent, so it isn't hard to follow Naomi's shape to the entrance of our tent.

As we stand in front of the tent Naomi points west. "Look!" It isn't necessary to say another word. Two helicopters are flying about two miles away, their blinking lights and constant rumble making them easy to spot. They seem to be flying in a circle, spitting out glowing red streams of light onto the ground below them.

"What're they doing?" I ask Naomi. "Are they shooting? What's that noise?"

"They're shooting niggers."

Naomi and I immediately turn around in surprise to face Holly standing behind us. "They're out there in the southwest part of Watts," Holly continues, sounding cold and hard. "The city hasn't knocked down all the burnt-out houses yet. Black people – or *looters* as the government calls them – are coming in there at night and taking windows, plumbing parts, anything they can sell on the black market. That's how they're surviving. These are the people who were burned out of their homes and live in the tents. But the government says they can't come in and take their things. The city brings in convicts and has them pile up all the junk, and it just sits out there doing no one any good. Since it's too big an area to patrol on foot, the police and Army patrol it by helicopter. With machine guns mounted in the choppers, they shoot at the people taking that stuff.

"So much for the love-thy-neighbor shit the President is preaching. Good night, you guys." Holly reaches out and squeezes my arm rather hard. Then she turns and disappears inside our tent.

"Well, White Boy," says Naomi with a deep sigh and a moment's hesitation, "I think we've got our work cut out for us. This is one crazy place. Holly must feel terrible knowing the Army is shooting at people who were once her neighbors and friends."

I feel like I'm in shock. "This whole thing seems unreal to me. I only hope we can do some good while we're here. This all seems way over my head."

Naomi and I hold onto each other for several minutes, then turn to go back to our bunks. I glance one more time towards the helicopters that have now stopped shooting, hearing only the rumbling as they fly around looking for more prey. I shake my head in disgust, and Naomi and I walk back to our tents.

Sleep eludes me at first. Then I find myself drifting in and out, half dreaming/half contemplating. Helicopters shooting at people! People trying to tip over our bus. Then I am back with Tim Smilich at age fourteen. He had been in my class and in the community about a month when the first fight broke out. He was definitely a bully. We would walk into our classroom and he would push and shove his way into getting the best seat or be the first in line.

I didn't personally see the first fight. I was outside class loading pottery into the kiln when it happened. I heard he and Shawn Laydon really got into it, right in the middle of a discussion on self-esteem. I guess it must have really pushed his buttons, so he decided to take it out on Shawn, who was a lot smaller. Fortunately, no one got hurt because Bonnie, our teacher, broke it pretty fast.

The second fight was the big one, and I had a front row seat. Tim was big for his age, about five foot eleven, 190 pounds. His opponent was Bobbie Pacheco, who was about five foot six, 130 pounds... after a big lunch. I was walking into class with Bobbie when Tim, who was standing in the doorway, spit on Bobbie and called him a dirty Mexican. He then proceed to tell him he needed a good scrubbing to get the brown stain out of his skin.

Now Bobbie had lived in the community for several years and he was a pretty calm guy. He just looked at Tim for several seconds and then casually told him to chill out. Before anyone knew what happened, Tim hit Bobbie right in the nose, leaving Bobbie flat on his back in a pool of blood.

I don't know where Philip even came from, but suddenly he was all over Tim and they went down on the floor in a heap. By that time the rest of us came out of shock and pulled Philip off Tim. But then there was Bobbie out cold, lying flat on the floor with his eyes rolled back in his head. We had never had a fight in school before, or for that matter in the community that I knew of, so to see Bobbie out cold on the floor shook us up pretty good. We didn't know if he was dead or not.

Someone got Diana, our Safety Inspector (we don't have a police force), and she stopped the bleeding and started treating Bobbie for shock. The rest of us brought wet towels and tried to help out however we could. Within a couple of minutes she had Bobbie sitting up in a chair. Boy, were we all relieved!

The next couple of weeks were kind of tense. Tim didn't come back to school or even talk to anyone. The rumor went around that he and his foster parents were thinking about leaving the community.

68

Then one day Philip grabbed me after school and said it was about time we start walking our talk – that if we really believed this love thy neighbor stuff, we better start practicing it. He then dragged me over to Tim's house.

Now Tim wasn't too glad to see us, and he acted pretty sullen, but eventually he asked us in. The conversation was pretty superficial at first. Then out of nowhere Tim started talking about his real dad and mom. He told us how they were both alcoholics and that his dad would use him as a punching bag when he got too drunk. Two hours later we were all in utter silence, and here was this big kid with streams of tears rolling down his puffy red cheeks. We all knew things would never be the same between us again.

Tim came back to school the next day and apologized to Bobbie. He then shared his story with the whole class. I think everyone really appreciated his courage, and it set a new level of intimacy and honesty for all of us. Tim and Bobbie became really close friends, and Tim is now studying to be a social worker at Middletown.

That was my whole experience with violence before this trip, so to actually see one human being shooting at another, even from a distance, is sickening. Don't they understand we are all ONE deep down? The fear that is running rampant in this country seems to me like the Plague during the Dark Ages. Where will it all end?

# Chapter 6

We arrived in Watts one week ago today. This first week has been somewhat uneventful. We've been stuck in and around our tents the whole time for security reasons we still don't completely understand. We're not allowed to venture out into the burned area of Watts or the surrounding neighborhoods. Police officials tell us it is too dangerous for us to leave our compound. There are over 2,000 community members from our co-ops here now and close to another 1,000 members of Habitat for Humanity.

Philip and I are sitting at a table by ourselves quietly eating lunch when an older-sounding gentlemen with a southern drawl comes up directly behind me and asks if there's room for one more.

"Sure," I answer automatically, not even fully turning around. Philip, sitting directly across from me, has stopped eating his sandwich and is staring off to my right. His face has gone blank, but his eyeballs have gotten so big they look like they're going to pop out of the sockets and roll down his cheeks. I realize something is not right about this picture, so I turn my head to my right and find myself face to face with former President Jimmy Carter as he sits down next to me.

"Hello sir," I hear Philip say with a catch in his voice. "My name is Philip Dacus."

"Hello Philip. My name is Jimmy Carter and I am glad to meet both of you boys." He then takes his spinach salad and apple pie off his tray, sets them on the table in front of him, reaches over and shakes both of our hands.

Tongue tied, I have to force myself to open my mouth and say, "Hello sir, I'm Jason Mann and I'm really glad to meet you."

"You boys, just call me Jimmy. Everyone else does now days." His smile almost touches both ears. "You as tired of waiting around here as I am? I'm ready to get to work and help these folks build some of these tire houses I've been hearing about. If we're going to have to wait around here, I'd just as soon be fishing." He looks intently at Philip, then at me; his furrowed brow makes his skin look like a roadmap I had once seen of New York City. "You fellas know anything about fishing?"

"Sure do," Phil answers before the question even registers with me. "Jason and I are fishing fools. Where we grew up, we fished for trout or catfish in the creeks and ponds around our homes almost every other day."

"Mmm, I love catfish," President Carter says straight faced while licking his lips. "Bake them covered with peanut oil for about twenty minutes and then dip them in peanut butter, It doesn't get any better than that."

Philip and I look at each other briefly across the table. He squishes his face and shrugs his shoulders and I roll my eyes, both of us hoping our new friend doesn't notice.

"You know," Mr. Carter says between bites, "I've been trying to get the local gendarmes to let me go fishing over at the beach. It's only seven or eight miles away, but they say the fish that are left are so contaminated, they're not even fit to make into catfood. Guess that reactor in San Luis lighting up and spilling its juice a few years back pretty well finished off an already polluted fishery along the Southern California coast." President Carter shakes his head and continues "But then I guess it's not really much worse than anywhere else in the country.

"Between the crazy weather radiating from the greenhouse effects and the disintegration of our ozone layer every year, I guess we've screwed things up enough that it's going to keep you younger folks busy for a long time... trying to clean up all the mess. If Congress had passed that Kyoto Treaty in '98, we wouldn't be so bad off. But politics, power, and money have ruled the roost too long. Congress chose to take the easy way out, and the American public went along with it. Now we're all paying the price.

"Oh well," he says as he takes his last bite of salad, "I believe God gave us the burning bush approach, like in San Luis Obisbo. But we didn't pay much attention, so now He has decided to use the two by four approach and see if we start getting the messages.

"Well, it's been good talking to you fellas. I've rambled on long enough. Got to get going on my after lunch walk. Ten miles is a pretty good chore for an old guy like myself. Good-bye, boys. I hope I'll be seeing you real soon."

As soon as Mr. Carter is out of sight, Phil and I immediately jump up and head towards our tent to tell everyone about our chance meeting with an ex-president.

Thirty minutes later, Marv walks into the sitting area in front of our tent, where seven of us are still sitting around and talking about Philip's and my talk with Jimmy Carter.

"These city officials don't have a clue what's going on here," Marv barks. "I just had a two-hour meeting with the city and county officials. They still have no idea what we're going to do here or why the President even sent us." Marv paces back and forth, his fists clenched, his face turning the color of a ripe tomato. "These government people seem to know how to send helicopters up in the air to shoot at people, or throw homeless people out of vacant houses, but they have no idea how to fix things to make them better. I've got to get some fresh air," he announces and hurriedly steps out the tent flap.

I didn't know Mild-Mannered Marv, as he is affectionately referred to, could get so upset. I look around the room. Everyone seems to be at a momentary loss for words.

"I think Marv is right." Philip takes up where Marv left off. "The city seems too disorganized to do anything right now. They keep bringing us more tires, but they don't even know why they're doing it. I suggest we hold a group meeting and decide what we want to do, and then let's do it!"

"I agree," says Naomi. "I'm tired of waiting."

"Me too," adds Irene. "Let's do it first thing in the morning when we're all fresh and calmed down. Then we won't make any mistakes."

"How about us, guys?" Luella asks. "Do we get a vote... even though we're not official community members?"

"I can't imagine why not," says Jess. "It seems to me we're all in this together." Everyone looks at one another, and for about twenty minutes everyone voices their views and approval. It's then decided that tomorrow morning we will make a group decision with everyone's opinion on what we are to do.

Early the next morning, Holly whispers, "White Boy, wake up!" After a brief pause, she tries again. "Okay. Would you, Jason, please wake up?"

I am still too tired to respond when a pillow suddenly hits the back of my head. I manage a tired smile from the top bunk over to Holly, who is staring at me intently while lying across her top bunk. "You're sure finicky," she says wrinkling her face at me. "*White Boy* is not a good enough name for you this morning."

"Yes, it's good enough," I answer in a whisper. "Actually I am beginning to like it. I just wanted to know if you knew my real name."

"I know your name: Jason; though you may never hear me say it again. It might ruin my image if I didn't call you White Boy. But be serious for a minute. I've got a question to ask you – a real big one – at least it's big for me."

"Go ahead. I'm an early-morning person, so I'm at my best," I mumble as I continue to wipe the sleep out of my eyes. I grab my watch off the top of my locker. It's 6:16 a.m. I hear other people already stirring, but I know we have another 44 minutes before we have to be up. I figure if Holly can actually turn serious on me, even for a minute, her question must be important.

"Well, it's like this. You know as well as I do that the mission we're supposed to undertake is impossible without a miracle. I mean, the odds are a thousand to one against us rebuilding Watts into a model of love, decency, and environmental integrity. Why, no one even seems to know where to start, or what we're to do. So why are you really here? Are you expecting a miracle, or don't you know any better? I am not badgering, Jason. I'm serious. I really need to know what you expect to happen."

At first I'm at a loss for words; it's a heavy duty question. I try to formulate my thoughts to make sure they make some sense.

"Holly, I do expect to rebuild this part of your city, and I expect it to be better than any part of any city in America. This is our mission – this is what we're focusing on. Even when we get discouraged, we've learned not to give up. When we met you guys in Sacramento, that was all part of the plan. It's about trusting our intuition, having faith in what we're doing, surrounding ourselves with people who give us energy, and then going for it."

"But Jason, you guys started your community over fifteen years ago. Times were simpler then. The country was together more back then. You weren't in a depression. You didn't have as much violence."

"I think things were getting bad even back then," I say. "My dad always told me that's why the founders started our community – to serve as a model to show people there is a better way. I think we've proven it works. It took more faith and perseverance for them to start out in the cynical '90's and build communities than it does now to rebuild yours. Now, at least, we know it works; and people are more apt to change when they're desperate – and they're certainly getting desperate. We know that much."

"White Boy, you're starting to sound like a preacher again, but I guess I'm getting used to it. But how do you act out of love when people are screwing you over or taking advantage of you? Aren't you worried about getting screwed over, being here trying to help when no one even cares?"

"Screwed over by whom, Holly? I am here because it's my choice, one hundred percent. People only hurt *themselves* when they try to take advantage of you. If I keep loving and give up attachments to all these things people cling to, no one can hurt me. If I'm not attached to my car, no one can hurt me by stealing it... that is if you have faith that something just as good or better will be provided for you after it's gone. Hey lady, I've already met you, and that seems like a benefit to me."

"White Boy, how did you ever get so much wisdom – or bullshit – for a guy your age?" Holly says as her face turns slightly peach-colored. "You talk like you're a wise old sage in your eighties, not like a boy going on twenty-one. How did you get so smart? Did you take smart pills in your community?"

"Holly, I'm not particularly smart, that's for sure."

"Take his word for it," says someone from the other side of my bunk. "I used to be his teacher in his fifth year." It's Marv, laughing. "Sorry to eavesdrop on you kids, but you were getting pretty loud. But Holly, we do try and teach – in our schools and through life in our community – how to be happy, to think, to try to be wise. We aren't concerned with our students being competitive with some other country or one another. We strive to have our kids turn out to be good human beings who know how to find joy and love; through that process, we believe, comes wisdom. So yes," laughs Marv again, "Jason does have a lot of wisdom for a person any age.

"Sorry kids. You keep right on talking. I am going to climb in my closet here, finish getting dressed and mind my own business."

Holly and I smile while continuing to stare in silence at each other My thoughts have slowed and I've run out of words. The sound of helicopters flying overhead shakes the tent but doesn't break the spell. Holly is very quiet and seems contemplative as she stares at me. Finally she breaks our silence and says very softly, "Jason, you are very wise, but I just hope that with as much hate as there is in the whole world, you are right. I've seen enough suffering to last a hundred lifetimes, and I don't need to see any more."

She leans over her bunk and puts her arms around me, giving me a very gentle hug. Her tears are warm against my cheek. I'm afraid she might fall out of her bunk, but she holds tight. We hold each other for what seems like many minutes, then release one another. We both seem rather shy and awkward afterwards.

Words do not come easily for me after our embrace, and my heart feels like it's beating twice as fast as normal. We get down from our bunks on opposite sides and dress in silence.

"Hey!" Philip bursts into our tent, breaking the silence. "Everyone wake up. Police and Army troops are every-where! Choppers are circling above. Something big's going on. Come on, hurry up, Jason. You're going to miss it."

Marv, who's already dressed, quickly heads out the tent door. I'm right behind him trying to tie my shoes as I walk. Outside, I see him talking with a police officer by the headquarters tent. In less than a minute he turns on a dime and comes back to where many of us are now anxiously waiting outside our tent. "The President herself is going to be here this morning! She's going to speak to all of us in about an hour, right here in Watts."

"That's what we've been waiting to hear," cheers Philip. "It's about time. The President! She'll know what we're supposed to do."

We literally stampede back inside to finish dressing. Suddenly, we care about what we look like. "What do you wear when you're going to listen to the President of the United States?" asks a wide-eyed Irene as she stands in front of her open dressing locker. At age seventy, she's seen a lot of things, been to a lot of places, but never had to dress to see a president.

"Oh, go for the red blazer," Naomi says as she bends over and madly digs into her footlocker, clothes flying in all directions as she burrows. "I remember last December when you wore it to the Winter Solstice Ball; you looked very elegant. You had all the men following you around like lost puppies."

Holly, sitting on her bed staring at her open footlocker, whines loud enough for the whole tent to hear. "I don't have a thing to wear but old raggedy blue jeans, T's and flannel shirts."

"Oh honey, don't fret," Irene shouts across the tent. "I've got enough clothes for all of us, and I'm not as old fashioned a dresser as you might think. You look like a size 8, and that's my size. So come on over and jump right in."

"Great!" Holly yells as she dashes across the floor to Irene's side of the tent. "So cool!" She claps her hands and does a little jig as Irene pulls out a bright yellow sundress and hands it to her.

"Hey Luella," shouts Naomi. "We're about the same size. You can borrow my pink jumpsuit."

I sit on my bed with my chin on my palm, in total awe. I've never had any sisters, but thought I was used to being around girls. But nothing prepared me for this – a dozen women wildly running everywhere in all states of dress and undress, surrendering the privacy of their dressing lockers to exchange clothes and chatter.

After fifteen minutes of total bedlam, Holly rushes up to me. She sounds out of breath. "The President of the United States right here in Watts! I can't believe it. Can *you* believe it? I guess you guys weren't exaggerating when you said she had personally asked you to come here. Maybe this whole thing is for real. Come on, Jason, hurry up, would you?" she nags. "Let's get out of here. I want to be right up front."

"I've been dressed for fifteen minutes; I've been sitting here waiting for *you*," I tell her in disbelief.

"Oh, you're so... picky, White Boy." She grabs my arm and drags me out the door.

The morning is slightly overcast, a light fog drifting in from the nearby coast. We sit down for breakfast, and Holly is immediately on all of us to hurry up, but we refuse to let her badger us; it still takes us twenty minutes to eat a breakfast of fruit and cereal. Then we're on our way to hear the President speak, Holly still complaining we took too long!

City workers have set up a temporary stage on the back of a large flatbed truck in the parking lot. It's right where we first got off the bus when we arrived. Police and soldiers surround the truck at every angle.

It almost seems like a dream; it's all happening so fast. Holly, Naomi, Philip, Melissa, and I all joined up at breakfast, and we are sitting cross-legged on the ground, right up front, not a hundred feet from the platform where the President is to speak.

Suddenly, a black limousine drives up and stops behind the flatbed truck. A large group of men and women, some dressed in suits and some in uniform, swarm the limo. A dignified black woman steps out of the limo, and they escort her up the steps of the truck. "It's the President!" shouts Melissa. The President looks over and waves as she quickly walks up the steps to the stage. Most of us get our first live view of a presiding President of the United States.

"It's her!" squeals Holly. "It's really her! My mom is never going to believe this!"

President Mandell is a short, slightly plump lady in her mid-fifties. Her coal black hair is darker than her cinnamon colored skin, and she is dressed modestly in a light blue suit. Her face is dominated by a broad, radiant smile. She stands behind the podium with her hands clasped and resting upon it. She doesn't quite look like what I expected of a president; but when she begins speaking, my perception instantly changes.

"Ladies and gentlemen," she begins in a firm yet compassionate voice, "first I want to salute all you volunteers for being here, and I want you to be the first to hear my ideas. I am here to give you the short version of my plan to save the United States of America. I won't bore you with the long version; I'll save that for my fellow politicians. They can suffer through it with me. We're here today to talk about... No! We're here today to DO something about the disintegration of our nation and its people.

"No greater peril has ever threatened our nation than what we face today. Our country, simply put, is in decay. For over thirty years the rich have gotten monetarily richer, and the rest of us – the majority of us – have gotten monetarily poorer. Also, unfortunately, many of us have gotten poorer spiritually and morally. In these areas, there's been little discrepancy. I'm going to briefly recap what is happening to our country, and then I'm going to tell you how I think we have to fix it.

"At this point in our history, more than 80 percent of America is owned by 11 percent of the population, primarily large corporations. About 78 percent of our income is received by 19 percent of our population. Right now we have 12 percent unemployment. Almost half of us live below the poverty level set by the Department of Health and Welfare. Medical expenses have gone out of sight, and we still don't have national health insurance for the 50 percent who don't have any medical coverage. Since the credit card collapse, only 4 out of 10 Americans own their own home. Sixty-one of the companies on the New York Stock Exchange don't produce or manufacture a single thing in this country. Twenty-three of our major cities are bankrupt.

"Our homicide rate is quadruple that of Europe. Domestic violence has become the norm in American society. Child abuse, both physical and sexual, is an epidemic. Thirty-three percent of our adults are alcoholics or drug addicts. Our divorce rate is 56 percent. Our jails hold over 4 percent of our population, and that figure could be 10 percent if we had the room.

"Environmental disintegration is engulfing the world, and we still produce 55 percent of the world's pollutants. Seventy-six percent of Americans polled in a national survey last month said life was neither fulfilling nor happy.

"I've heard the common complaint that many of our citizens feel their primary importance is that of a consumer. Spend, spend, spend – that's what we're here to do, keep the economy going. Well, the credit card and Stock Market Crash got rid of that vogue. But people still want and demand a change – a dramatic change. I think it's been a long time since people have felt fulfilled, since there's been a sense of joy in the world.

"That's the bottom line – our end product. I could go on for another hour about the problems, but what's the point? I'm not running for office; I'm in office. Every president for the last fifteen years has been politically castrated and left impotent. We have to turn things around; if we don't, total chaos will prevail and our government and society will completely collapse. Make no mistake about it. It will totally collapse; we're very close to it."

The President momentarily stops and looks at the audience as a teacher might her class. Satisfied they are paying attention, she continues. "As President, I have a Ten-Point Plan which I believe can turn this country around. It is not a cure-all, but if followed, it can lead us in what I believe is the right direction. I will make it simple and straight. I'll ask Congress to pass my whole agenda within four weeks. If this does not happen, we will have a national referendum on these issues. If the public votes for my agenda and the Congress does not pass it, then I will ask that each congressman and senator who voted against it resign, be impeached, or be recalled. If my platform is voted down in a national referendum, I shall resign and the Speaker of the House will take over. This may seem radical, but we absolutely have no choice at this point.

"My plan, simply put, is as follows:

"Point One deals with law enforcement and has four parts. First, we will leave the state of emergency and martial law in effect for one year from this date. We will totally ban all assault guns and semi-automatic weapons. Anything that is not a legal hunting weapon or a handgun designed for self-protection will be illegal anywhere in the United States of America. If we have to change the Constitution then, by golly, that's what we'll do.

"The second part of Point One is that we will revamp our prison system to rehabilitate and educate felons, instead of just locking them up. We know too well that now when they get out of prison, they commit more crimes because they're dysfunctional and unemployable. We'll open halfway houses in every state, to move prisoners back into society in a productive way that will be a win-win situation for everyone. Acts of violence such as sexual abuse in the home, especially against children, will be prosecuted the same as other violent crimes. Felons will be held accountable for the crimes they commit, but society must be held responsible for rehabilitating these offenders and breaking the cycle of abuse where it starts – in the home. The idea of pure retribution without rehabilitation has been a total disaster and has almost bankrupted the country, both monetarily and morally.

"The third part of Point One is to organize a worldwide, citizen-based boycott of all violent movies, books, music, or any type of entertainment that encourages violence or sexual abuse. I know this again may seem radical, but our backs are up against the wall. I will personally lead this boycott, and you will hear me speak of it and plead for it every day I am in office. It's about time we take responsibility for what's going on.

"The fourth part of Point One is that the government will pursue any violent gang, cult, or racist group with every method at its disposal. Our armed forces and the FBI will assist local governments in every way possible. We will not put up with any more hate groups in America.

"Point Two: We will immediately put into effect new environmental regulations. (A) All polluting vehicles of any type will be banned from our roads within two years. We've had ten years to prepare for this, and we're not going to wait any longer. (B) We will ban all toxic waste dumping or sewage dumping anywhere not previously approved for such use in the National Environment Code adopted last year. No body of water, including the oceans, shall be an acceptable location for dumping. (C) No more farm land in the nation shall be covered up or destroyed for any purpose. (D) All new dwellings built must be totally energy efficient and have their own source of energy. Also, we'll ban coal and oil as heating or energy producing sources. Energy credits will be given to homeowners or investors who convert their existing homes or commercial property. (E) All fresh water shall be recycled and reused. (F) All clear-cutting in what little is left of our forests shall be banned totally and immediately from the date this proclamation is signed. We will also ban all raw wood exports from both private and federal lands. We will also turn the Forest Service back to the Forest Service and get it out of the political arena. Lastly, we will sign the new Bellrose, Honeycut mining law, and the updated Kyoto Treaty, which has been languishing for fifteen years.

"Point Three: We will raise the minimum wage of all workers in this nation from where it has been for ten years at $6.50 per hour to $12 per hour over a two-year period. This act alone will pump $162 billion into the economy and $40 billion into new sales tax dollars. Our studies have shown that there are very few companies left in this country actively competing in the overseas market but paying less than $12 per hour. This raise will thus not significantly impair their ability to compete in foreign markets. This act alone should raise almost half of our nation out of poverty. We will ask for a two-year wage freeze on each individual making more than $200,000 per year. We will ask for a voluntary cut of 25 percent of wages for all athletes, physicians, corporate heads and their subordinates who make over $250,000 a year. If people aren't willing to do these things voluntarily, then the government will intervene. We need – no, we MUST – dramatically shrink the discrepancies of income in this country, or we will have outright revolution.

"Point Four: We will revise the tax code – by simplifying it – and make it more equitable. There will be a national 10% sales tax. Every item that is not food or a legal drug will be taxed at 10%. Individuals making under $250,000 will pay no other federal taxes. Individuals making over $250,000 will be taxed at 50% on everything above the $200,000. Businesses (whether individual or corporations) will be taxed at a simple 25% of net profit. There will be reductions in net profit by deducting direct expenses for company medical premiums, childcare expenses, and energy-saving remodels, or those sums given to stockholders who transfer their stock to employees. The IRS will no longer exist as we know it today. For those of you interested, we have our plan available in much greater detail. Just ask my Press Secretary.

"Point Five: We will bring home all troops from foreign soil within two years, except those in the United Nations service. We will continue to strengthen the United Nations and the role it plays in disarming the entire world. We will continue the process of eliminating nuclear weapons to reach the goal of zero weapons by the year 2020. We will reduce all full-time military personnel and bases by 50 percent over two years. All military personnel being terminated will be given the option of going into federal job programs to help rebuild our American cities. We will require every person at the age of 18 to join (without pay, for one year) the National Guard, Peace Corps, or Federal Job Corps. The idea is to rebuild our cities and countryside and to affirm the importance of service.

"Point Six: To reduce our budget deficit, we will abolish all agricultural subsidies. In the year 2009, one hundred forty million dollars was paid out in this category alone. The role of the Department of Agriculture will be to help farmers produce better quality and quantity of products without the use of chemicals and pesticides. We will totally abolish the Departments of Education, Transportation, Commerce and many smaller departments. These duties will be turned back to the states where they belong.

Regarding education – we're going to turn the educational system back to the states, counties and cities. But the Department of Human Sciences will be a resource for the states and local school districts to look at education as a way of raising healthier, more balanced, children.

"Point Seven: We'll form the new cabinet-level Department of Human Sciences whose sole purpose will be to study and enhance how we humans are going to survive on this planet in a positive, loving, ecological, caring way in the 21st Century. We have gotten to the point where we must spend more energy and money on how people are going to live and enjoy life in the 21st Century than we do on new technology, new weapons systems, and consumer toys.

"Point Eight: We will provide free medical coverage for every person in this country. Employers will provide coverage for every employee and his or her family. In return, the employer will be able to not only claim medical premiums as an expense, but also as a write-off against income. The employee will not have to claim these premiums as income. There will be a two-year moratorium on raising any medical costs. Monies awarded for medical lawsuits will be limited to costs of direct expenses and damages.

"Also through Point Eight, we will make sure every human being in this country has the opportunity for two healthy meals a day regardless of whether or not he or she is willing to work. After all, we do that for our pets, animals in zoos, and any other hungry creature. That's the least we can do for any human being. We can do this through direct subsidies of food and sending job program employees to the Salvation Army. The monies for this program will come from the elimination of all agricultural subsidies that directly pay farmers not to grow crops.

"Any able-bodied person on any federally funded welfare program not working towards getting a job or learning skills will have their benefits terminated by the end of next year. Every person has a right to food, medical coverage, and a job if they want to work, but we will no longer pay able-to-work people to stay home and collect welfare. Nor

86

are we going to pay women to stay home and have babies. The nation can't afford it and neither can the recipients. It's about taking personal responsibility; but that responsibility goes two ways. Society must create equal opportunity for all, whether it's a homeless person or a welfare mother. But individuals have to take personal responsibility for themselves, and take advantage of the opportunities given them.

"We will guarantee every person the opportunity to have a job. Zero percent unemployment in two years is our goal. Federal Job Corps in every state will train and provide work for every American willing to work and unable to find work elsewhere. We will provide tax savings credits against income for companies creating new jobs and hiring new workers. This will reduce the income received by the federal government but will be made up by savings from the elimination of the Departments of Commerce, Transportation, and Education.

"Point 9: By giving three years of tax-exempt status, we will encourage any new or old company to become all or partly employee-owned. We will give direct tax credits against income or sales tax to stockholders of companies that make this switch for losses they may incur. Basically, shareholders can trade stocks for tax credits. The employee-owned company then will pay the government back over ten years for these tax credits.

"Point 10: The last and most important point is why I am giving this speech here in Watts in front of the new Peace Corps members. It's a bit ambiguous compared to some of my other goals, but most important. We will form our new Peace and Job Corps, along with our National Guard, to be the most important government entities in our lives. One by one, we will enter every American city and town and rebuild it for people – not just for profit or for egotistical reasons, but simply for the people who live there. You will see new, environmentally sound communities designed for both people and the earth. You'll see new parks, recreation and cultural centers, and new businesses where the profits are more evenly distributed and the work more rewarding.

"We're going to have to learn to live more simply on this earth and to live less selfishly. When I meet with Pope Daniel next month, I am going to tell him he and the Church are inadvertently helping to destroy the earth, and God's creations along with it. We're simply filled up, folks. We've got to put up the *No Vacancy* sign.

"Our new motto for the country is going to become 'Love thy neighbor and the earth as thyself.' It may sound religious; it may sound sappy and naive. But, you know? I don't care. It's what we're going to have to do if we're going to survive. There is simply no other choice. We've finally reached that wonderfully delicious point where our backs are up against the wall, and now we have no choice. We must act; we must change the way we're living.

"It's going to be up to the women in this country to show their feminine side and say it's okay to love and care for one another. Women, it's time that you stand up and say 'bullshit' to all the wars, violence, poverty, overpopulation, and greed. We need to take the best of both sexes – to offer and combine them instead of just relying on masculine traits – to guide us.

"Somehow, through the ages, I think the best that women have had to offer – the feminine traits of love, compassion, and faith – has often been overruled and overshadowed by fear and greed. It's time we take these positive traits and make them the basis of our new society – our new family and community units. Remember we are ONE; we're all in this together, and so let's act together.

"This afternoon we shall start to rebuild Watts, and tomorrow we shall rebuild the rest of the country, if for no other reason than for the sake of our children. We must try to be what we hope our children will become. If we're not there to be positive role models, who will be? May peace be with you. Thank you."

There is utter silence for about thirty seconds after the President's speech. We are all stunned. Everyone, from the police to the Habitat for Humanity people, just stand in silence. Then, of course, wild applause erupts, lasting for at least ten minutes. No one has ever heard a speech like this from any president in the history of our country.

The question that seems to be on everyone's mind is, "Okay, it sounds great, but now what do we do?"

# Chapter 7

Walking back to our tents, Philip, Holly, and I are all deep in our own thoughts, unable to express our feelings on what we've just heard. Naomi is not with us, having gone to the headquarters tent with Marv to get the reaction of local government officials to the President's speech. Crowds of community members and Habitat people filter through the compound on the way back to their tents. Some sound like they're talking about the President's speech. Others, like us, walk in silence as if in shock.

Philip is the first one to speak as we enter our tent door and sit down in the front living area. "That was a great speech! Just the way I like it – short and to the point."

"It *was* a great speech," I concur, "especially the part about the new Department of Social Sciences. It's about time we got our priorities straight."

Holly says, "I like the part about getting something done, that we're going to make some changes – especially here in Watts." Philip and I nod our heads in agreement.

Other people straggle in the door and the conversation turns to the subject of when we are going to get started rebuilding Watts, and how are we going to do it.

The speech has stirred our emotions and fueled our energy. We sit and talk about how we're ready to go to work. The word is that someone from someplace is going to be here shortly to tell us what we're supposed to do and where to do it. Our conversation drags on before I realize several hours have gone by, and all we're doing is sitting in the shade of our tent. Not a thing has happened.

Finally, Naomi blows through the door like a gust of angry wind. "Guys," she begins excitedly using her and Holly's favorite word, "there's *no one* coming to tell us what to do. I just came back from headquarters. Marv is still over there, but everyone's in a quandary. The President's on her way back to Washington, D.C. Now, no one here wants to stick his head out and make a decision on how to get started. Actually, no one seems to know for sure exactly what we're supposed to do."

Holly and I are sitting across from each other. She looks over at me, frowns, and then says, "Don't look at me, White Boy. I just live here. You're the guys who got the President's order and came to help." She pauses for a moment, cocks her head in reflection, and then goes on in a more conciliatory tone. "But you know, maybe we're just supposed to go out and get started and not wait for the bureaucracy. We need to take action. Somebody just has to take the lead. Why not us?" She looks around the tent. "Doesn't look like anyone else is going to do it."

Jess quickly speaks up. "I think Holly is right. We just need to get started. We could wait around here forever. I think we should pick out a spot on one of those empty streets and just start building a new community today. Right now."

"I agree," says Brad. He's one of our engineers but still not much older than Naomi. "The tires are already out there. There's glass, lumber, wiring fixtures. Most of what we need is in the piles scattered around. We can build cabinets and doors out of scrap lumber. I say we build an earthship and let the rest of the people see what we are doing. I guarantee that will get their attention, and maybe even motivate them to help."

Irene again suggests we have a formal group meeting and come to a consensus, but it's obvious to the rest of us that we've already *reached* consensus and are ready to go to work. We just needed a direction, and now we seem to have found it. We all look at one another and then at Irene. "Okay," she says with a laugh, "let's go for it."

One by one we walk out of the tent door into the California sunshine. We go over to the piles of shovels, buckets, wheelbarrows, and other tools left for us by the city cleanup crews in hopes that someday we would get started doing something.

We walk through the burned-out streets of Watts, five and six abreast. The word spreads as we walk and sing, and our group keeps growing. Brad, who seems to be taking the leadership role at this time, leads the way. He had managed to do some scouting about of the area by befriending some of the Army combat engineers. He's been the only one of us able to spend time outside our immediate vicinity getting a feel for what needs to be done.

We walk together in a group for about a quarter of a mile, ending up at a corner of two burned-down streets. Desolation. No trees, no cars – nothing but piles of crushed concrete from the fire and stacks of tires left by the county. Across the street, older stucco homes still stand. We're close enough to actually see people moving around inside the houses. I see a man peering out of a window and a lady looking out her screen door. They watch us parade back and forth trying to decide where to start and what to do first.

"I believe that's a good place to start," Brad says as he points towards a lot that looks like it once hosted a corner house. Now there is only a pile of black concrete next to a slab foundation. "I've been told this is the corner where the first fire started – I deem it an appropriate place to start rebuilding." Brad kicks the dirt as if to make a point.

This time we form a group right there in the burned-out street. All of us sit down together and hold hands, only needing five minutes of silence for the energy to pass between us. Then, ready to go to work, we start grabbing tools and tires. Having chosen the lot, Brad drives four wooden stakes into the ground around the perimeter where we want the corners of the new house. We can use the existing foundation and just add on where it needs to be extended.

"Brad, what are we going to use to fill our tires? We have only a little sand," asks Brian, another young engineer from Higher Ground.

"I've been thinking. We can use all the crushed material from the burnt houses. It's burnt, but that doesn't matter," says Brad, running his hand through his thick black hair. He points to a pile in the distance that looks like dark-colored sand. "There is a lot of crushed concrete. The city has had people pulling out all the wire and everything else that doesn't belong, and those big rock crushers the Army's been using can pound those large chunks of concrete and stucco into powder. It may work better than sand. We'll pour water on it; hopefully, it will be like concrete again. You won't be able to knock it over with a Caterpillar tractor."

"Sounds good to me," says Brian enthusiastically. "Let's try it."

Soon all 38 of us are hard at work. Some pass tires to a team who sets them on the ground. Another group pushes wheelbarrows containing crushed concrete and dumps it into the tires. Fortunately, there are still city water mains to the sites, and we are able to tap into them. Holly gets the job of hosing down the powdered concrete that has been dumped into the tires.

Working together, we're happy. Some of us sing as we work; others work in silence. Some banter and joke, but we all work, and the afternoon goes fast. In no time, it's 7:30 p.m. and we're all exhausted. Sitting and lying around the work area. most of us are too tired to do any more. We've made a start. There's a row of tires three high around the perimeter of what will be a house.

"Let's clean up and call it a day," Brad calls out. There's a weak response of "Hallelujah" from some of us, and one by one we start standing up and putting our tools in piles.

We walk back to the mess hall in a ragged, disorganized procession, like a tired but not beaten army. Black beans, fish, and rice never tasted better. We literally limp back to our tents after dinner.

"That's certainly the hardest I ever worked," says Holly as she plops down on top of her bunk. "What have I gotten myself into? And my mom thought *I* was a masochist. Well, I guess I'm in good company." She puts her pillow over her head and moans and groans some more.

"I agree," I say as I try to find a comfortable position for my aching body. "It's the most work I've done in quite a while."

"It's almost 9:00," Naomi says with a groan. "We were at it from 2:00 to 8:00, but it seemed longer than that. Building tire houses is hard work."

I do remember Holly and Naomi talking, but the next thing I know my alarm clock is going off. As I try to raise my head off the pillow, I can barely make out that it's already 7:00 a.m.

"Is that your alarm, White Boy?" says Holly in a groggy, threatening voice from her bunk. "If I weren't such a polite, sweet girl, I would tell you where to stick that thing."

"Oh, I'm so sore," complains Naomi from below. "I wish we could go back to sleep. I need my rest."

I sit up in my bunk expecting more abuse from Holly when Philip, fully dressed, walks happily into our tent whistling some bird song. "Come on, little birds. Everyone wake up. Chirp, chirp, chirp. Time to get going. Remember, the early bird gets the worms."

"Oh, shit," says Holly as she picks up and then throws her pillow at Philip. I follow suit, and my pillow hits him in the chest. He keeps smiling but soon everyone in the tent is tossing a pillow at him. He retreats out of our tent under a barrage of pillows and a chorus of catcalls.

"What's got into that boy?" Holly grumbles as she starts climbing out of bed. "I thought he was the one who liked to sleep all the time?"

"I think it's the stimulation of all these new female friends he is making," laughs Naomi. "I think he's overly stimulated!" Both girls break out in a fit of laughter, but I just shake my head. That just went right over my head.

I'm having a tough time moving and end up being the last one in the men's latrine. By the time I'm dressed, Holly and Naomi are already waiting at the door.

"White Boy, you sure are slow," chides Holly. "It's supposed to be us girls who are the slow ones, but in this trio we've created, you're the procrastinator."

"Aw, quit picking on the poor boy," quips Naomi as we all walk together over to the mess hall. "It's okay, Jason," she continues. "We still love you, even if you are slow." She pats me on the back again like a lost pet, then she and Holly join in another orgy of laughter.

We arrive at the mess tent, a large green canopy with several dozen wooden tables underneath. The canopy sits right in the middle of what must be a hundred tents, all replicas of the one we live in. The cooks have another small canopy adjoining the larger one where they do the actual cooking. There's been half a dozen cooks working for the Army who've been rotating doing the cooking for all our community members. They have been really good to us, knowing many of us are at least partial vegetarians. They've worked to completely cut red meat out of our menu. This morning, breakfast is bran cereal, oat bread, and fresh fruit. I don't think it hurt the cooks' feelings that many of the foods we like do not require much preparation or cooking. It has certainly been less work for them.

It takes us about forty minutes to finish breakfast. We believe in mindfulness when we eat – that it's important to honor all that we put into our bodies. So mealtime is not something we rush. After breakfast we're on our way back to the job site – ready, if not quite eager, to get back to work.

We have spectators. The word must have gotten out throughout the neighborhood adjoining our work area that some crazy people are out here stacking up tires on top of each other for no apparent reason. By 11:00 we have several hundred spectators watching us from across the street.

With 38 people at work, the tires are going up fast. Brad has borrowed a green-camouflaged front-end loader and driver from his Army friends. That makes picking up and dumping the crushed concrete go much faster. We have all four perimeter walls up on our first house. I'm sure it looks strange to the neighbors to see four walls of tires sitting on an empty lot.

I am shoveling powdered concrete into a wheelbarrow inside our earthship when I hear, "Hey, White Boy, what're you building here, a bomb shelter?" This is a male voice, not Holly's. I look but I don't see anyone talking to me. "Over here, White Boy, on the other side of your tires." I climb up to the top of the tire wall I've been working on and peer down at a tall, thick-chested, bearded black man peering up at me.

"Hello," I chuckle. "We're building tire houses, not bomb shelters."

"Tire houses?" the bearded man laughs.

"They're cheap to build. Just need lots of labor. They're also cheap to live in." I make myself comfortable on the wall of tires and soon find myself giving my whole earthship pitch to him, plus ten other black men who have come from across the street, their curiosity getting the better of them.

97

"Well, White Boy, who's going to live in these houses anyway? Why do you folks want to come down here and live right in the middle of Watts?" one of the older men asks, obviously baffled.

"I wouldn't mind living here, but these houses are going to be for you. We're building them for the people who got burned out during the riots."

The men look at me with puzzled faces. "Why are you building for us?" one asks. "The government paying you lots of money to do this?"

"No, we're here as volunteers from Oregon. Others have come from all over the nation to help."

The men still look puzzled and even a bit suspicious. The tall, thick-chested man who has introduced himself as Cliff asks, "Why would anyone come to Watts from Oregon to help rebuild our city for no pay? It doesn't make any sense. You folks seem like nice people, not convicts, but I for one think you're either crazy or some type of religious zealots." Cliff turns and starts to walk back towards the street.

The rest of the group follows his lead, all ambling back across the street together, shaking their heads as they talk among themselves. Soon I see them talking to their friends across the street. There seems to be much talk and debate; I don't think they quite know what to make of us.

I get back to work, my break over. It's getting hot already this morning. It must be around 85 degrees. We work until noon and then take a lunch break eating cheese sandwiches, carrots, and fruit from the sack lunches made for us by the Army cooks. Making chairs out of tires, we sit in the sunshine, discussing what we've done.

I have a good feeling going through me, like a natural high. There isn't much smog today; the sky's a pale blue with long white streaks running through in a dozen different directions. It looks like a gigantic chalkboard with chalk lines going through it.

Our lunch hour goes too fast, and we get ready to go back to work. I see we have a new group of visitors walking over from the direction of our tent sites. Members of other communities and people from Habitat for Humanity must have gotten bored with waiting for leadership from the government. A half dozen men and another ten or so women walk up to us and ask what's going on. We talk to them as we work, explaining who we are and why we're out here.

They start pitching in. By the time we quit at 6:00, we have thirty more volunteers and the promise of many more by morning. Fortunately, some of them have had experience with alternative building materials.

That night as we again lie exhausted on our bunks, Holly, on her back with her arms spread-eagle, looks over at me and says, "White Boy, you didn't tell me the work was going to be so hard − 'specially the twelve-hour days. You folks always work so hard where you come from?"

"No," I answer as I roll over on my stomach and prop my drooping chin up with my hand. "We're just excited to be doing what we are doing. Six-hour days, five days a week is what we are used to, unless it's *really* important. But this situation is an exception. When you're doing something you really like or feel is worthwhile, it's amazing how much extra energy it gives you."

"I noticed your name, White Boy, is catching on," Naomi says from her bunk below.

"Yeah," Holly says, "and looks like you made some new friends today. Those men were okay. They weren't from any gangs or posses, just wanted to know what was going on. Even though they made fun of us, I think they like what we're doing. I just hope none of the local posses start to bother us. I guess they'll leave us alone as long as the Army is here. But this is their turf, even if it is burned down. Makes me feel a little spooky."

Totally exhausted, I eat a few of my crackers and try to keep my eyes open, but "spooky" is the last word I hear as I roll back over. I am on my way to dreamland express where morning will be the next stop.

"Naomi, is that you? You remember what the corporal said about eating in bed? Naomi? Naomi, is that you?" I rub my eyes but just can't get them to open. It must be three or four in the morning. "Hey, somebody's eating. Would someone please answer me?"

"Jason, this is Naomi. What are you waking me up for? I am exhausted, and I don't eat in my sleep."

"Somebody's eating, Don't you hear them?"

"Jason, the noise is coming from your bed. You must be talking and eating in your sleep. Go back to sleep. Please!"

*I am awake,* I think, *but I am not eating. Got to open these eyes. What the heck are those red eyes staring at me from the end of my bed? This has got to be a nightmare!*

"Geez," I scream. "Oh my God! Help! Please help me!" It's a rat! Gotta kick it off. "Geez!"

"Ah... Ah... Shit! Shit!" Holly yells. "Jason, you threw a rat at me. God, where did it go? Jason! I think it's still on the end of my bed."

"Holly, I didn't throw that rat at you. I just kicked it and it flew off the bed. It's gone. I don't see it on your bed."

"I can't believe you did that! Jason, that's the worst thing anyone ever did to me in my life. God, you're horrible."

"Calm down everybody. You two just relax for a minute," says Naomi as she shines her flashlight around Holly's bed.

"I can't believe this. I think that rat peed on my bed," Holly whines. "It's all wet down here."

"I am really sorry, Holly. I didn't mean to kick him on your bed."

"Jason," Holly says, "you're just lucky there's an extra empty bed next to me here or I'd be sleeping in your bed.

And I guarantee *you* wouldn't be there with me. Now good night both of you. And Jason, don't ever talk to me again."

Good night everybody," laughs Naomi, "Sweet dreams."

I rub my eyes and pick up the tent flap to peek out. The sun is up high in the eastern sky. I must be running a little late. *Wow, what a nightmare I had last night. Wonder where everybody is. Guess they must have gone to work already.*

A note's taped to the end of my bed: "I hate you. You'll pay for last night. Holly."

*Great!* I think to myself, she must really be mad. Rolling out of bed, I start to get dressed. I move as fast as my body allows, but slow down as I grab a bite to eat. As I head over to the building site, I wonder why no one woke me up.

I'm almost there when I stop short. Naomi, Philip, and Holly are all standing in a circle in front of me. Behind them must be at least 2,000 people, milling around like they're waiting to go to work. I take the several steps over to where my bewildered friends are standing. I find myself stuttering, "Who are all these people? What's going on?"

"The rest of the new Peace Corps must have gotten tired of waiting. They all seem to be here now," Naomi says, obviously still in total awe.

"Yeah. Also, it looks like a lot of the black folks from around here don't want you honkeys building houses for them without their help," Holly says proudly. Then she looks directly at me and gives me a dirty look. There must be 500 black neighborhood men and women who have crossed the street and look eager to get to work.

"Hey, White Boy." I look around and there's the tall older man I talked to yesterday, Cliff. "You guys gonna put us to work or just stand there and talk? You know you white folks can't build all these houses by yourselves. They'll turn out much too white. You need some color in them." He laughs loudly. "So just tell us where to get started."

"Just a minute, don't go away," I yell back. *'Where to get started? My God, I have no idea.* "There's Brad over there," I say to Naomi and Holly. "Come on. Let's see if we can give him a hand."

The three of us make our way through the crowd to where Brad and several other of our engineers are talking and waving their hands about in an attempt to get organized. We join in the pow-wow and soon find we're giving directions and helping to form work parties. It's an unbelievable task, but we start by grabbing fifty people at a time and get them started on a house. Then we grab fifty more and start another. I see more men than women, but the women jump right in, doing everything from stacking tires to pouring cement.

By evening, some semblance of order has been restored. Now instead of one house going up, there are thirty. The Army has sent over six more front-end loaders and five dump trucks to help speed up the process of getting materials to the sites.

By 6:00, I am again exhausted. We are finished for the day and get ready to leave. I notice ten or eleven soldiers milling around looking at our unfinished earthships. A thin black man who looks about thirty and wears a camouflage soldier's uniform walks over to Marv and Brad.

"I'm Corporal Sullivan." He points to the soldiers who are still looking through our first unfinished earthship. "Me and my friends over there are off work now, and we want to help." He seems almost apologetic. "We can set up lights and work on those spaceships all night, if you just show us what to do."

Brad smiles, looks over at Marv. Marv shrugs his shoulders and nods. "Sure, why not," Brad says.

We can use all the help we can get. Even though we're tired and want to go back to camp, we're excited to have their help, so we spend another two hours helping the Army volunteers getting started building spaceships... I mean *earth-ships*.

Later that night as we lie in our bunks, Holly turns to face me, her own face flushed like she's been crying. "Well, White Boy, I am still mad, but it does seem like a miracle is going on out there." Her voice quivers slightly. "I wouldn't have ever believed it could happen this way. Why, there was even a cop out there today helping me set tires. Said he worked nights and had nothing else to do during the day. You know what? He was a white boy – a white cop out here on his own time helping to rebuild Watts. I guess it must be a miracle. Well, good night, you guys. I better shut up before I make more of a fool of myself." She makes a noise like a sob, rolls over to face the other direction and pulls the covers over her head.

"Good night, Holly," I reply quietly, not knowing what else to say. I too pull my covers up under my chin and close my eyes.

"Good night," pipes Naomi from below. "I love you guys."

# Chapter 8

Brad's at his wit's end. His stocky frame stands erect and confident, but his face is flushed and his eyes narrowed. The two of us stand in the middle of what was once a street. About 2,500 people are scattered up and down the block – stacking tires, hauling concrete, building trusses, and looking for guidance.

"Jason," he confesses in a tired voice, "I'm in over my head – 30 earthships going up at once! It's just too much. Look," he points in the direction of three black men walking towards us from across Hayward Street. "There are more people coming to help all the time."

Sure enough, more people from the surrounding neighborhoods and the refugee tent city are streaming in from every direction.

"We have to get more organized," I tell Brad. "We need to divide our people who have built earthships before so there are a few working on each house. Right now some house sites don't have anyone who's ever built one before, and we have to run back and forth giving advice. Plus we need a plan. We're just putting houses up where we know there was a street. We've got to figure out how we're going to keep all the houses facing south, so the solar systems will be facing the sun."

Brad's quiet for a moment, scanning the bedlam in front of us. "You're right, Jason," he blurts out as if waking up from a trance. "Tonight after work we'll sit down and get more organized... or we'll go crazy. We'll do the best we can for the rest of the morning."

More people keep arriving, and Brad and Marv are kept busy assigning them to work sites. Philip and I walk up and down the streets making suggestions, acting as go-fers and helping out wherever we can.

By 2:00 the news media has gotten the word on what we are doing. They seem to be arriving as fast as our helpers. Everywhere I look, someone from a T.V. station is setting up a camera or a news reporter is asking for an interview.

A tiny, dark-haired woman in a lavender jumpsuit and a matching beret, followed by a burly man carrying a large camera on his shoulder, follow me around as I show new workers what we are doing. "Oh, sir," the lady says as she catches up with me. "I am Stephanie Carlos from KTLA here in L.A. You're the only person that I've run across who looks like he knows what he's doing. I wonder if you would give me your name and just a couple of minutes of your time to let the people of L.A. know just what's going on here."

"Me? I'm Jason Mann," I stutter, looking into her pleading, coal-black eyes.

"Yes, sir. You are one of the foremen here, aren't you?"

"I don't think so. I mean, we're all doing this together. No one's really in charge. Brad and Marv are the ones you might want to talk to though. They're leaders right now."

"Right now? You don't have regular leaders or bosses?"

"No, ma'am. We just pick them when we need them. See right over there?" I point. "See two guys standing there with about a hundred people standing around them asking for directions? Those are the guys you want to talk to."

While she is looking in dismay at the crowd gathered around Marv and Brad, I duck into a group of men and women pushing wheelbarrows full of concrete, then head over to the crew working on a nearby earthship.

"This is one wild jungle," exclaims Holly from behind me as I, with my hands on my hips, try to decide what I should do next. "This place is a zoo!" She laughs as we rub elbows. "There must be 300 news people hanging around! White Boy, you sure look perplexed, or maybe overwhelmed is a better word. That pretty woman scare you, asking all those questions?"

"No, I just didn't know what to say. I've never been on T.V. before – haven't ever watched it, except in the middle of winter. So I figured I'd just duck out." Holly just keeps smiling and shakes her head as she hands me half a Snickers.

We sit back against the tires on the house I was near, eat our candy bar and survey the situation. It's an amazing sight – thousands of men and women, even some children, going in every direction looking totally unorganized.

"This looks more like a party than a work site," Holly says.

There are thirty unfinished earthships, still looking more like stacks of tires than houses. But somehow houses are going up. The job is getting done.

"Look," laughs Holly. "There goes Naomi on a golf cart." Sure enough, Naomi has commandeered a golf cart from somewhere and is weaving through the workers, a small cloud of dust trailing.

"She's delivering water." I say, noticing the plastic milk jugs piled five deep in the compartment behind her.

I point to the original house that we started working on, down at the end of the first row. "It's almost finished. Brad found two unemployed electricians from the neighborhood and they're just now putting in the electrical work. It's a trick to get the hang of running wire through walls made of tires and sand. This morning they just looked at us with their mouths half open as Brad explained what needed to be done."

Back in my field of interest again, I'm on a roll. "We're also desperately in need of more glass for the solar panels on the south side. This house's dimensions are thirty by sixty feet. The entire sixty-foot south side is a ten-foot deep, almost separate glass room. This will be the solar collector and green house."

I think I've lost Holly's attention but go on anyway. "We're going to need a solar vortex system for each house. Each house is going to produce its own electricity. The greenhouse will provide heat in winter, and the thick tire walls will keep it cool in the summer when the greenhouse is closed off. But to produce its own electricity, the house will have to have an active solar system, and we will need to find a lot of them."

"White Boy, you're getting too technical for me. I'm gonna catch up with Naomi and get a drink, then go back to work with the *laborers*," she says in mock sarcasm. She gets up and looks me in the eyes momentarily but this time doesn't smile. She just twists her lips sideways, tips back her baseball cap and then walks back towards Naomi, who is delivering water to the people working two earthships down. I watch her leave, her hips swaying as to music. *What an interesting girl. She's definitely her own person. Getting kind of hard to take my eyes off her. Hmm...* I grab a shovel, take another glance at Holly talking to Naomi, and then start to help shovel concrete into the stack of tires in front of me.

It is after 6:00 again when we quit work for the day. The Army people (there must be 300 of them by now) with their floodlights are starting work already, and some of the T.V. people are still here shooting footage for the news.

About ninety of us have gathered this evening to formu-late a plan. Most of us are experienced at building earthships, are engineers, or are experienced in the construction trade.

The Army and the police have each sent a representative to help us make decisions regarding logistics. It's 2:00 in the morning; we've been here since 7:00 last night and there's still a lot to be done.

We have come up with a bold plan to turn Watts, street by street, into a model community that will rival any of the planned communities we've already built. The streets will be divided in half. One half will become basketball, handball, and kickball courts. We'll tear up the other half of each block and put in crested oat grass, a new blend of drought-resistant grass with deep roots discovered at Cal State just last year. This grass can survive on the scant five or six inches of rain a year that L.A. now averages. Here we'll build picnic areas, volleyball courts, and baseball and soccer fields.

Cars will be limited to using the alleyways behind the houses. Fortunately, these older neighborhoods already had alleys.

For each one hundred houses we build, we'll build a common house or rec room complete with cooking and dining facilities. It'll be up to the people in the community how  they use this building, but it will be here for them. In our community we share meals four or five times a week. We hope some of these folks will get ideas on how we do things.

Our plan should take roughly two years to complete, depending on how many workers stay on the job throughout that period. We hope to build 5,000 earthships by the time we're done with the whole project. It will be the largest community of its kind that we know of, and we hope it will be an example for the rest of the nation... and the world.

We've decided we'll break into thirty groups – three experienced earthship builders to a house. This will facilitate the building of each structure. We'll ask more of the local people to form groups to go to the piles of material left from the burned houses and bring us back anything that is usable.

The Army and police have given us permission to do this, so we don't have to worry about getting shot at.

We've done what we can to get organized. I return to our tent knowing that I will only get a few hours of sleep. Tomorrow we face the Herculean task of organizing thousands of people – and tomorrow is only a few hours away!

Six a.m. comes too soon. As I peek out of my tent flap, I see the sun is barely over the tips of the San Gabriel Mountains to the east. The sunrises here are eerie, the sun pushing its way through the brown haze that's engulfed the city for three days.

Holly and Naomi are already dressed and cleaned up by the time I literally roll out of my bed and stand, groggy-eyed, looking for the bathroom. "Well, White Boy," says Holly as she looks at me, her hands on her hips, "that's what you get for going out and partying all night with your friends. We got to take nice hot showers last night. The Army Corps of Engineers finished building our showers and bathrooms yesterday. They hauled away all those yucky old outhouses, and now we don't have to take sponge baths anymore. Hallelujah. We were in bed by 9:00, and you were out partying all night! Shame on you."

I turn my head away in disgust and ignore the harassment. Naomi and Holly both laugh as they walk out of the tent and head towards the chow line.

I sit on my bunk for several minutes trying to gather energy. Looking across the room, I see Brad is also just climbing out of bed. Step by step I get dressed, then head out for some breakfast – just realizing that I never got dinner last night.

"Jason is that you?"

"What?"

"Jason, I'm Tony Bender, your half brother," a tall slender blond haired boy of maybe seventeen says as he walks up to me and puts out his hand.

"Hi," I reply, shaking his hand but too stunned to say anything else.

"We saw you on T.V. last night. Mom recognized you. I never would have known it was you, since I've only seen your picture. She's waiting in the street in our limo; she asked me to find you and bring you over."

"Okay," I say, still in shock. "Lead the way."

"Wow! It was tough getting in here," says Tony, chatting away a mile minute as we walk. "But you know Mom – she just told those soldiers that she was one of Mayor Franklin's closest supporters and they finally let us in. "So Jason, what're you doing here? How much you getting paid? Isn't this project lined up with that crazy woman in the White House? Dad thinks she needs to be assassinated or at least locked up. He's a big supporter of Speaker of the House Quail, and he figures if we get rid of her, then Dan is in. I sure hope he's right."

"Slow down," I tell Tony, "You're talking way too fast for me." Then I take advantage of the pause to try and briefly explain to him what I'm doing here. But as we walk up to our mother's long, gray Cadillac, I realize he's not taking much of it in.

"Jason, I am so glad to see you," says my mother as she invites me to sit next to her in the plush back seat. No hug, but a polite kiss on the cheek is our greeting. My mom's in her mid-forties, still quite pretty with her perfect auburn hair and camel colored eyes. But her delicate girlish face looks a little tired and is covered with what looks like a thin layer of plastered on white paste.

A Plexiglas partition separates us from the front seats. I can see Tony and the driver, but I can't hear them. Nor do they look like they hear us.

"Well Jason," my mother starts in, "it's been a long time. What a surprise to see you on the news last night. I told Tony that we needed to get over here and immediately rescue you from this god-awful place. You need to come home with us and spend some time. But we can talk about that later.

"I'm sure you're dying to hear all the news about us and what we've been up too. Of course, Bill sends his love. Like always, he's working at least sixty hours a week and it's so hard for him to get away from the office. His firm is representing Mayor Franklin in the upcoming bribery scandals that I am sure you've been reading about. Bill is now Franklin's most trusted advisor. I must say, it's a very prestigious position.

"Of course, Tony here is doing wonderfully. He's still boxing, and Bill got him a full athletic scholarship to his alma mater, Greighton. That's going to really help out on our finances this year." Mom goes on for another ten minutes about their wonderful life, then she gets back to me coming to stay with them.

"Now Jason, you've got to come see our new house. It's old Victorian and is almost 7000 square feet, plus the maid's quarters. We've got plenty of room. You could come live with us and we could be one happy family. I promise you'd never be bored as we've got a boat, motorcycles, and plenty of cars. You name it and Bill has bought it. And of course, a liquor cabinet that would rival most bars. It would be good to have you there, Jason. That big house gets a bit lonely sometimes and, to be honest, Bill and Tony both drink a fair amount when they're around. It would be great to have someone sober, besides our maid Charo, to talk to when I am home from the office."

"Mom, I don't think so," I answer instantly. "I really love what I am doing and the people I am working with. Besides, we're doing something really great, something that's going to make a real difference in people's lives."

"Jason, Jason, you sound just like your father, a head-in-the-sky idealist. You do know, don't you? That's the reason I had to leave him. He was always trying to figure out some scheme to save the world. And look at what it got him! You two live in some commune in Oregon in a house made of tires! I look what we have compared to him and it just saddens me the way you must live. "Jason, you could have everything we have." Tears now roll down Mom's eyes. Suddenly, she puts her arms around me and gives me a stiff embrace that smells like a mixture of perfume and alcohol.

*What to say? I don't want to hurt her feelings but need to tell her the truth, straight out.* My chest feels tight, like it's going to explode. I know deep down I love her, but I need to get out of here.

I reach for the door handle. "Mom, this is where I belong. I'll write you in a couple of weeks and explain more about what we're doing here. But I've got to get to work now. My friends are expecting me."

Our eyes stay connected for another moment as another tear runs down her left cheek and then a desperate, almost despairing look darts across her face. She starts to open her mouth, then closes it again. I slowly lean over and give her a kiss on her wet cheek, open the door and wave one last time to Tony.

*Oh, my God!* I see half the town at our site. They must have seen what we are doing on T.V. last night. Thousands of them are here to help, watch, or maybe make fun of us. White, black, brown – they're all waiting to be told what to do, waiting on *us* to lead, and we aren't trained as leaders.

Brad and I look at each other and he puts his palms up in the air. "Jason, we've got to round up everyone we can find from the meeting last night. We'll have to regroup. You go to the left and tell anyone from the meeting to meet back here in twenty minutes. I'll go to the right and do the same."

As we make our way through the crowds, we find about eighty of the ninety people who met last night. Brad tells us, "Well, we really have our work cut out for us. Each of you put on a white armband to let people know who you are. We have plenty of material and at least 5,000 workers. We'll split up and work on 45 houses at a time, then start on the parks and fields."

Every team of two grabs about a hundred bodies and starts on an earthship. "Irene, you and Brian should start asking around for maintenance and landscape people, and we'll start on the first parkway. It'll be chaotic for the first couple of hours, but it should smooth out by this afternoon. Good luck!" Brad waves, almost like he's giving the group a salute.

We scatter ourselves among the mob and start to organize what we can. It takes several hours to get crews working on each house, but by 10:00 a.m. organized chaos has again descended.

We get several hours of work in before being confronted by our next big obstacle. About a dozen portable outhouses arrive from the Army Corps of Engineers. I go over to the street to help unload them. We've just taken the first one off the truck when a gray electric Oldsmobile sedan with a City of Los Angeles emblem pulls up to the curb next to us. Two police cars follow.

A lone man in the Olds steps quickly out of the car and connects with the four police officers. They briskly walk up the sidewalk and into our earthship community. I follow behind to see what's going on.

"I don't know who's in charge, but I want this work to stop!" shouts a short, middle-aged man in a buttoned-down, dark blue, pinstriped suit. He's trying to be heard over the noise of thousands of people working. He looks around to see if he has been heard. "Get me a bullhorn!" he shouts to one of the four police officers standing next to him. "That's the only way these people are going to hear me."

The officer shrugs his shoulders, says, "Yes, sir," then goes back to his car. Within several minutes he's got a bullhorn.

The man in the suit resumes shouting, this time in the bullhorn. Still, hardly anyone can hear him, or at least pays any attention to him. "Give me your gun," he tells the officer to the right of him. "This will get their attention." The officer looks reluctant but takes his revolver out of his holster and hands it to the man.

"Be careful, sir. It's loaded."

"I know that, Captain. That's why I want it!" The man raises the revolver above his head and quickly tries to pull the trigger three times, but nothing seems to happen. He keeps on pulling the trigger, but the gun is still quiet.

"Sir," a red-faced officer says and then whispers something in the suit-man's ear. He pulls the gun down, pushes some kind of button, and then raises the gun back in the air.

Two loud explosions echo in our ears. Everyone as far as I can see has stopped working, looking toward the spot where the shots were fired.

After a moment's hesitation, people – realizing that they're not being shot at –start walking cautiously towards the man to see what is going on. "My name is John Culver, and I am the City Engineer for the City of Los Angeles," he shouts into the bullhorn. "What you people are doing is totally illegal. You have no plans, no permits. Most important, you've paid no fees! Everything you are doing is against the law! I will have any man, woman, or child who continues to work on this mess arrested immediately. Now disperse." Culver takes the bullhorn away from his mouth, puts his hands on his hips and scans the crowd for their response.

After about twenty seconds of utter silence, a young black woman shouts, "This is our town. This is our neighborhood. We can rebuild it if we want, and we do want to! You can't stop us!"

"I *can* stop you! And believe me I will!" he shouts back into the bullhorn. "I will arrest the first person who does any more work here. Now disperse! That's an order!" Culver is flushed, breathing hard; sweat glistens on his brow. He puts down his bullhorn and mutters, but loud enough for me to hear him. "I am an appointed official, and I am the law. These people better learn now to obey the law... or else."

The police officers standing next to him look at one another, faces tense, bodies stiff. They don't look pleased by the possible confrontation. No one makes a move to leave, and Culver starts raising the bullhorn back to his mouth.

Suddenly, two older men (one black, one white, both gray-haired and about 85) step out of the crowd. The black man walks over, bends down and, as if in slow motion, picks up a medium-sized tire. Without saying a word he hands the tire to the other man who, with some effort, sets the tire on top of another tire already in place. The black man slowly bends over, picks up a wooden-handled shovel that was left lying on the ground, and starts to shovel dark, crushed cement from a nearby pile into the tire.

Many of us recognize the men, and a hush envelops the crowd. I look back over at Culver. He looks dumbfounded, but only for a minute.

"Officer!" he bellows to the Captain standing next to him. "Arrest these men now! Immediately!"

"But, Mr. Culver," the black officer says, "we can't do that! That's Ex-President Carter and the Reverend Jackson!"

Sweat now drips off Culver's entire face. But I have to give him credit, for he seems stunned only for a moment. He looks to be in his mid-forties, so he's probably heard of these men but had no idea what they looked like. He straightens himself up and shouts at the four officers. "I don't care who they are. They're breaking the law, and I want them arrested – now!"

Anxiety's written across the Captain's face. He shows no intention of arresting a former President of the United States, even on the order of a city official. In fact, he probably isn't sure right now if his men will even do it, especially considering the angry crowd they'd face. I've noticed some of his men have been coming down here on off-duty hours and helping out, so I doubt if they have much empathy for Mr. Culver.

"I am sorry, Mr. Culver, but I cannot arrest these men without a warrant. And, sir, we don't have a warrant." The Captain doesn't say another word, turns, and stiffly walks away, trailed by his three men.

"I'll have your jobs for this!" bellows Culver. "You men over there, you soldiers." He points to the Army equipment operators who have stopped working and are watching the drama. "Arrest those men now! That's an order!" Culver appears to be breathing really hard, his face the color of a ripe beet. In contrast to his raving, the soldiers sit on the buckets of their front-end loaders, smile and chat amongst themselves.

Finally, one of the Army officers, who looks even younger than me, walks over and says, "Sorry, sir. We're under direct order of the President of the United States. She told us to do whatever was needed to help the people working here. She said nothing about arresting them, only helping them." With that, he turns casually away and barks at his men to get back to work.

The soldiers shrug their shoulders and, with grins still on their faces, climb back on their seats. One by one, they start the engines of their noisy machines, eroding any chance of Culver again being heard.

Chaos reigns again; people are back to work.

A few people give Culver dirty looks as they walk by him, some from our community offer a friendly smile. Most just ignore him, like he was never even there.

Slowly, as if in a trance, Culver turns around, walks toward his car, gets into the gray Oldsmobile, rolls down his window, looks back towards us one more time, and shakes his head. Then he drives off... in the direction of the L.A. freeway.

I find myself actually feeling sorry for Culver. He acted as if his whole importance as a human being was in his job as City Engineer, his self-worth tied to the power that he thought that position carried!

I turn my mind back to the job we have to complete. My eyes wander over the site in front of me and rest on Holly and Naomi. They're stacking tires on the earthship going up two ships down from where I stand. Both are wearing cutoff jeans t-shirts, and matching maroon colored baseball caps. Naomi is brown from all this California sunshine. Holly, with her black skin drenched in sweat, sparkles in the sun. *Holly's a kick, certainly unlike any girl I've ever met before. I wonder if I am...*

"Hey, Jason! You look like you're in a dream standing there. What's going on?" asks Philip as he walks up behind me and puts his hands on my shoulder.

"Hi. I guess I'm just daydreaming... about life, and about girls."

"Well that's kind of new for you, Jason. You usually leave that job up to me. But it's about time you started thinking about girls. So who are you dreaming about, Holly or Naomi? Or both?" We both laugh.

"Good question. I guess I don't know. I mean, I know Naomi is a good friend, but with Holly, it's a little different. I can't put my finger on it, but I guess I will eventually."

"Oh, I'm sure you will, Jason," laughs Phil, wearing his normal spread-across-his-face grin. "I can almost guarantee it. By the way, I noticed Brad eyeing Naomi at lunch, so I'm glad it's Holly you're interested in."

"Hey, you boys going to get back to work or have you guys been promoted to supervisor?" Cliff walks up, a shovel in his hand and a grin on his face. He lives in one of the small houses across Hayward Street and I'm glad to have him as a friend. During the last couple of days I've really learned to like his dry sense of humor and his good nature.

"You boys are gonna turn into statues, you stand here any longer." Cliff puts down his shovel and stands between Philip and me, a hand on each of our shoulders. He's a big man, at least six foot five. I feel he could pick Philip and me up at the same time and move us anywhere he wanted.

"Yeah," he adds with a broad smile. "We'll just put a little of that concrete on top of you, pour on some water, and you two will be permanently enshrined here – a salute to all of you community members who have swept down from the North to help us rebuild Watts. Maybe you two could kinda get in an action pose though, as long as we're going through all this trouble."

Philip and I are both laughing as we walk back towards the earthships with the now poker-faced Cliff. It's been an interesting day, to say the least.

> A man who experiences no genuine
> satisfaction in life does not want
> peace. . . . men court war to escape
> meaninglessness and boredom,
> to be relieved of fear and frustration.
>
> Nels. F.S. Ferre

# Chapter 9

Four weeks have passed since we finished our first earthship. Now 126 of them stand done or nearly completed. The parkways are taking shape. Kids are already playing basketball on the courts. Our first community center is in the middle of being built and we hope to finish it next week.

Over 7,000 workers are on our site now – about 5,000 of them volunteers from around L.A., the rest from our communities and Habitat for Humanity. On the order of the President, the Army has sent in 30 earthmovers and 27 front-end loaders. Local construction companies have volunteered a dozen more. Watts is on the move.

Holly, Naomi, and I are taking a rare Saturday off. It's a warm sunny day; although it's close to 4:00, the temperature is still in the 90's. The smog is tolerable, but my lungs still gasp for breath. The nearby mountains are slowly going into hiding as the day wears on.

Naomi and I have told Holly we want to venture out into the parts of Compton and Watts that weren't burnt, to see what is going on and how the people live. Holly isn't sure that's such a good idea.

"You guys are so much into your intuition, and mine has an alarm going off. White people just don't wander around on foot in the tough black neighborhoods of L.A. With so many soldiers in town, posse activity has been quiet, but the word is out that many of them are angry over what we're doing in Watts. They fear they're losing control, and that they won't even be welcome in their old neighborhoods."

"It's okay," I tell her. "It'll be fine. I have a good feeling about this." But in reality, I hear the little voice saying, *Shut up, Jason. You don't know what you're talking about.* I tell the voice, *I'm tired of being so boring. I want some adventure.*

"A 'good feeling.' Oh, great, Jason. Now I'm really worried!" Holly says.

We've taken showers and exchanged our dirty work clothes for shorts, t-shirts, and sandals. Outside of the tent compound, we pass through our earthship community, waving to our friends still working. Philip looks over and waves back with an envious smile. He, Brad, and some of the others took last Saturday off and went to Disneyland, so they decided to work all day today.

Heading across Hayward Street, we find ourselves in the tiny, unburned portion of Watts. Kids in the street wave to us. Older folks in their yards ask us how we're doing. The folks living around Watts seem to recognize us as the kids who have come to help rebuild the city. Even though we may be the only white people in Watts today, I feel accepted. I feel very much at home as we walk along the sidewalk and cross into the city of Compton, like I've been here before. Most of the houses are in worse shape than I expected. Some of them have roofs where every shingle is arched towards the sky. How they could ever keep out the torrential rains that hit Southern California is beyond me. Cracked stucco from the earthquakes, peeling paint, and brown lawn from years of drought – none a pretty sight.

"Boy, these houses are really old," I mention to Holly. "They're like antiques, especially that blue one over there. The roof is dead. The porch is falling down. It looks like one of its posts has come loose at the foundation. I'm amazed it's still standing."

"Yes, they're old, White Boy. And as you can see, most of them are in bad shape. The doctors, lawyers, and investors who live in Bel-Air or the Valley own many of them. They never did put much money back into these homes. They're only in it for the money and tax benefits. Now, since the earthquakes and the fires, they don't put nothing back." Holly shakes her head in dismay.

"People should have stock in their own homes," Naomi tells Holly as we walk along.

Then Naomi stops dead in her tracks. "Say, Jason," she says, her wide open eyes staring me in the face. "We've been so busy working... Has anybody thought about or decided who's gonna own this community we're building?"

"I don't want to even think about it," I say shaking my head. "I do know the city's taken possession of the whole burned area by Law of Eminent Domain. Don't ask me what that means. They paid the owners something for the land, though I heard it wasn't very much. How they plan to divvy it up, I don't have a clue. Hopefully, they have a plan. Maybe the City Engineer has it all figured out."

"I'll bet he does," Holly scoffs.

"Somebody told me they saw on the news that he resigned," Naomi says. "Don't know who they put in his place, but he's got to be better than Culver. Although I have to admit, I think anybody doing that job would eventually have it go to his head. We shouldn't give anyone that much power or responsibility. It just feeds the ego. Responsibility needs to be shared."

We're lost in our conversation and have walked a couple more blocks when I hear Holly cry, "Oh, shit!" I look up the street and see two black, older style cars slowly heading our way. They are low to the ground, and both look like old gasoline engine types of 20th Century vintage.

"Let's turn around and head the other way," Holly says urgently, grabbing my arm hard. "Maybe they didn't see us."

"What's the problem?" I ask as I reluctantly follow Holly's request and turn around toward the direction we came.

"Listen, White Boy, those are posse members and we're doing three things wrong as far as they're concerned. First, we're on their turf. Second, you're two white people with a black girl; they probably figure you're just trying to pick me up and that Naomi's a lesbian. And third, you're just white! Some black people, especially posse members, plain don't like white people even breathing right now. So let's walk, and walk fast!"

"Let's go, Jason," Naomi demands as she grabs my arm. "If I'm going to be a lesbian, I want to live to see what it's like. This is Holly's home. She knows what's best."

*Okay. I guess that's instant karma,* I say to myself. *Say something bad about old Culver, and then we get trouble right in our face.*

We start walking in the opposite direction, as fast as we can go without actually running. I keep glancing back and see that the two cars keep getting nearer. We don't get hardly a block when both cars pull up next to us. We keep walking but watch them out of the corner of our eyes – not looking directly at either car.

Finally, one of the cars pulls farther ahead and one drops behind us a little. They both come to a stop, and several black teenagers with green baseball caps turned backwards, step out of the first car, walk over to the sidewalk and stand three abreast, blocking our path.

I feel dizzy; it seems like everything is going in slow motion. Looking around for help, I see people peering out of the windows of a house directly to the side of us. They're shaking their heads, as if not knowing what to do.

Up the street the three teenagers who were playing basketball and had waved at us make a dash for their house. For the first time that I can remember, I am totally panic-stricken. Things like this just don't happen where I come from. My legs are shaky, my whole body is sweating, my mind can't focus.

Standing directly in front of me and staring me right in the face is the oldest-looking boy, who looked about 18. "Where you going, White Boy, with these two fine women?" He's taller than me and has on a black t-shirt that says something I have no time to read. A chain hangs from his neck and some type of long, thin knife is in his hand. The twisted grin on his face tells me he isn't here to tell us how much he likes the job we've been doing.

"We're just out for a walk," I stammer as I take a deep breath. "We're working in Watts on the tire houses. This being our first day off, we wanted to see what the rest of the neighborhood looked like."

"Wrong answer, Jason," Holly whispers.

"White Boy, how come you have two girls, and we don't have any? These girls must like do-gooders. Maybe we should be do-gooders, and they would like us, too. Whatcha think, White Boy?" He laughs, putting his face so close to mine that I can feel the warmth of his breath against my face. Not known for being a *wise-ass*, I'll never know why I answer him with, "You never know. Maybe you should give it a try!" But that's what I say, surprising myself – and from the bug-eyed look on Holly and Naomi's faces, I guess them too!

"Wrong answer again, Jason," Holly hisses as she looks at me in astonishment. "You're going to get yourself dead if you go three for three."

"You're a smart-ass, White Boy, I can see that," interjects the leader, whose grin is turning to a sneer. "But I like you. You're okay. Got spunk. We'll just take your girlfriends for a little ride with us and party a little. Then we'll drop them off at your place tonight, and we'll all party." He laughs, throwing back his head slightly and showing off a mouthful of broken teeth.

I hastily glance to my side and see two other green-capped boys from the other car moving up from behind and slipping their arms through Holly's and Naomi's. Holly immediately pulls away, turns, kicks one of the boys in the knee and spits in his face at the same time. He slaps her hard across the face. She lets out a yelp and spits right back in his face. He grabs her again and twists her arm behind her, forcing her down on her knees.

I've never been violent before, never been in a fight, but my first reaction is to turn and grab her assailant by his shoulder and demand he let go of her. He does let her go, only to push me away while someone else kicks my legs out from behind me. I go sprawling across the sidewalk. I feel like I'm going to throw up but manage to struggle up to one knee.

"Get away," Holly screams. "You're gonna get yourself killed. Run away, Jason, or they're gonna kill you. Run!"

"Good advice, White Boy." The leader stands over me... knife in his hand. "But I'll just cut you a *little* this time." He waves his knife slowly in my face and grins. "Next time though, maybe I'll get my gun out of the car, and it won't be so nice." His face is a snarl now, the smile barely visible.

A posse member holds Naomi, her arms tightly pinned behind her. Then he screams so loudly that something inside me jumps. "That bitch bit me! She bit me!"

As I stagger to my feet, Naomi screams, "Let him go! Damn it! Let him go!"

I hear more yelling and, as I look up, I see an old man with a rake in his hand crossing the street towards us. "Let those kids go, now! You better let them go!"

"Get in the car," snarls the guy with the knife as he turns back toward Holly and Naomi. "You two women – hurry up! In the car!" The boys in the back grab Holly and Naomi by the hair and try pushing them towards the car, holding their arms behind them.

Suddenly, I find myself putting my head down and plowing into one of the girls' assailants. We go sprawling across the sidewalk in a twisted contortion of bodies. I try to get loose, but he's stronger than I am. We struggle, falling back to the ground. Everything seems to be in slow motion, like at a movie.

"What the hell is this?" stammers my assailant as he releases me from his headlock. Blurry-eyed, I look up and see the three black teenage boys who had waved to us while playing basketball. This time, though, they look like they're getting ready to play baseball or football since two of them have on football helmets, and all three have baseball bats in their hands. I stagger to my feet and behind them, coming towards me from across the street, I see a heavyset woman also carrying a baseball bat, her jaw set firmly and her eyes blazing. Everything is getting louder.

My wrestling companion, after letting go of me, gets to his feet. He looks around for his friends. Our would-be assailants now seem too confused to make a move. They stand together in a circle like a herd of musk ox entrapped by a pack of hungry wolves. I try to clear my head, figure out what's going on. Now I see people from all directions, coming towards us and yelling, "Get out! Get out of our neighborhood, you black trash!"

*Crash!* My head jerks around as a young boy throws a large rock at one of the black cars, smashing the windshield into little pellets.

When the posse members realize they're cut off from their cars by the angry pack of neighbors, they let go of Naomi and Holly and retreat down the street, yelling obscenities at the pursuing horde of at least twenty angry people. Another teenage boy runs up from the side, picks a large rock off the ground and hits one of the members in his head. The posse member looks around bewildered, then falls to the ground.

The posse leader turns back angrily, looking past his pursuers at me. He shouts wildly, "I'll get you some day. I'll get your white ass, I promise." He turns and runs, leaving his fallen comrade on the ground holding his head.

I stand with Naomi and Holly and watch in both horror and fascination as people from the neighborhood smash the windows of the posse's cars and beat on the fallen boy with their bats. A man comes out of his garage with a Jerry can of liquid that I assume is gasoline. He throws it over the top of one of the cars. Another man tosses a lighted newspaper on it and everybody runs, except the boy on the ground. *Vah-room!* There is a huge flash and explosion. Fire envelops the car and the battered body of the boy lying on the ground.

Suddenly, without any warning, Naomi springs into the street, streaks through flames and smoke to the boy's side. Without a moment's hesitation, she bends over then grabs the boy by his arms. In less than a minute, flames dancing around her, she drags him across the sidewalk into the front yard of the closest house.

*Bam!* A shot rings out and Holly grabs my hand and screams at Naomi, "Come on. We gotta get out here." We all start running down the street towards our camp.

We can hear sirens in the distance. I look back and see raging black smoke billowing in the air. We must run for three or four blocks before we finally stop. I gasp for air and start shaking uncontrollably.

"That was close," Holly says, out of breath. "Too close for comfort."

Naomi and I are speechless, having no words to describe what we have just been through. We all walk in silence back to camp, each too stunned to talk or even touch one another.

Finally, Holly breaks the silence, her voice still quivering from our attack. "Well, White Folks, you got a real taste of what it's like to live in the inner city – or any part of the city now." Naomi, herself still visibly shaken, puts an arm over

Holly's shoulder but Holly continues raging as she rubs her jaw. "I knew I shouldn't have taken you guys in there with me! Shit, we almost got killed. God, I hope my jaw isn't broken. People are angry out here. They want all this violence to stop, but stopping violence with more violence just makes it worse. They attack us; we attack them. There's got to be a better way. But, shit, my face hurts."

Seeing Holly holding her jaw, the tears running down her cheeks, I'm overwhelmed, I don't know what to say.

Our tents come into view as we cross the last street of houses before we enter our compound. A jeep with four soldiers carrying rifles passes in front of us. The drivers smile and wave as they turn into a gate in the barbed wire that separates us from the rest of Watts. As we walk, I stop shaking so badly, and I feel my voice coming back.

"Those neighborhood folks are angry all right," I say. "But the anger in their hearts is as bad as this madness in the streets. Both have to stop if there's ever going to be real peace. Did you see them beating that boy on the ground? They wanted to kill him, and maybe they did. Naomi, that was a brave thing you did, grabbing that kid like that." I again feel sick to my stomach.

"It was just instinct, Jason. I didn't even realize what I was doing. But what's it going to take? People have to start pulling together non-violently, saying 'enough is enough' — like we're doing in Watts by working together. We're going to have to be the catalyst for non-violent change. It's got to get better. I can't believe what we just went through. It's like my worst nightmare."

We stop and form a small circle in front of our tent and quietly hold each other tightly for fifteen or twenty seconds. Finally, with my voice still slightly shaky, I ask the girls, "Are you guys all right?"

"I'm better now, Jason," answers Holly. "I really like the way you guys give these long hugs. It really helps calm me down – gets me, as you say, *centered.*"

Naomi laughs softy, "Remember, Jason, we're supposed to be taking care of *you.* How do you feel?"

"I'm going to be okay. Actually, I'm really starting to feel calm as we sit here and I let go of the whole thing. Somehow though, we've got to get people to replace this epidemic fear out there with love. I know it sounds idealistic, but it's the truth. I can remember my dad telling me a story of what happened to him about twenty years ago. He had gone to a symposium in Aspen, Colorado, put on by an organization called Windstar. John Denver, a popular recording star in the 70s and 80s, founded Windstar. Denver made a song called *Higher Ground* in which he sang about going after your highest ideals, living life the way you truly believe it should be lived, and not compromising your integrity.

"Well, that's where our community name came from. Dad was at this symposium, and Marianne Williamson was speaking on the Course in Miracles, of which she was both a teacher and a student. When she was younger, in the early 1970's, she had been very upset over the Vietnam War that was going on at the time. She talked of the anger she was carrying around over it, and other things too – like environmental destruction. Anyway, after reading and studying the Course in Miracles, Marianne realized her anger had her just as stuck as the people making war and polluting the environment. Her perception of herself had been of peace, but the reality she had created was of hate and spitefulness toward the people with whom she disagreed. At that point, she decided the only way she could bring peace to the world was by bringing peace to herself first. She said that people at peace with themselves and their God don't make war or pollute the environment. Only angry people do these things.

The way to really change the world was through loving yourself and the people around you.

"Well, my dad heard her tell this story and it was like a light went on in his head. He realized he had been acting in the same way as Marianne – out of anger, not love. To hear him tell it, from that moment on his life changed. He started studying the Course. A short time later, he had a vision that he was supposed to be working on building a community. So he started following his intuition and within a year he met other people with the same outlook and vision; they became the mastermind group that founded our community. The really neat part for my dad was that he said for the first time he was at peace. He had the community as a support group for the rest of his life to help keep him in that space."

"Great story, Jason," Naomi says. "I didn't even know all that about your dad and our community. I guess I've taken a lot for granted."

"It *is* a good story," Holly adds. "It makes sense, definitely food for thought. Was your dad one of the founders of the other communities in your co-op?"

"No, he helped consult on many of them, but he wasn't a founder. Other people who shared my father's vision founded most of the communities. Many of them lived in our community and wanted to be pioneers to help create opportunities for more people to belong. You see, our communities were only designed for so many people. When we become full, it's time to start another one."

"Jason, you sure are a walking encyclopedia," Naomi jokes, her voice now calm. "But let's talk about something lighter. I am wigged out."

"Where is everybody else?" I ask. "It's 7:30 and the tent is empty."

"I think," says Naomi, "there's a play that the Habitat people are putting on tonight. But I'm too bushed, and I'm not going anywhere."

Soon Holly and Naomi are lying on their beds and are off on another subject, leaving me to my own thoughts. I lie on my bunk and listen to Holly and Naomi chatter about what seems like everything under the sun. It's like they've already forgotten about the attack, although it was only a few hours ago. I admit to being envious. Males at Higher Ground have learned to try to be non-judgmental, sensitive, and communicative, but as much as girls and boys are brought up the same there, the girls generally are more open and communicative, especially on subjects males often find boring. These feminine traits seem to make it easier to love and to become closer more quickly.

I've become even closer to both Holly and Naomi in the last few weeks. But they seem to have become closer to each other. I guess I'm a little jealous, but not sure why.

Sleep is almost here, and it's too hard to concentrate. It's been an insanely exciting but crazy day. I check for leftover crackers, roll over, pull my covers over my shoulders, and let sleep wash over me.

> The louder he talked of his honor
> the faster we counted our spoons.
>
> Ralph Waldo Emerson

# Chapter 10

We've been in Watts ten weeks now; our mission has gone well. We've built over 600 homes, 8 rec centers, and our park system is ahead of schedule. We still have over 5,000 workers building and scrounging for materials. Scrounging is becoming more difficult though. Most of the usable items from the scrap piles have already been used. We have lots of concrete, plenty of tires, and an abundance of labor; but we're starting to run short of everything else. We hope to build another 4,400 houses while we have the momentum, but we'll need more plumbing, electrical fixtures and lumber to finish.

The next issue to address is who is going to own the houses we build. The issue of who is going to run the community of Watts is also undecided. The Los Angeles city government is still operating in a crisis mode and, since Culver's visit, has seemed happy to leave us alone, as long as we don't bother them or ask for anything. The problem now is how to start asking for materials without having the city bureaucracy breathing down our necks again.

A coalition of black, brown, and white leaders from Compton and Watts has suggested that a new community called Los Miracles be formed. They say it should be totally separate from L.A. They presented the plan to the City Council but have not yet received a response. The problem is, L.A. still owns the land Watts sits on, even though they condemned it. Up until now, the City of Los Angeles has been very quiet on what its plans are for the land and the earthships we are building. We have acted on faith and the support of the President, but legally L.A. has the final say on what will happen to the community we are building.

As we wait for the City Council's response, members from the coalition are meeting with different members of our communities to pick our brains to get ideas that can be adapted to their new community. The dialogue and sharing of ideas impresses us.

As I let my mind wander, I stretch my arms out as far as they will go. I do the same with my toes. The sun feels great against my bare chest.

"Wow, these tires really reflect the heat," Naomi says as she puts her hand over her mouth to stifle a yawn.

"Yeah," Philip says. "It's the black color of the tires. It absorbs the heat like a sponge, then lets it off slowly, keeping everything around it toasty."

"All I know is it feels really good just to lie here on this pile of tires and do nothing for a change," Naomi says. "We work almost every day, ten hours a day. I need a vacation. I need to go back to Higher Ground and go to work just for a rest."

"I agree," Philip yawns. "I am tired too. I miss going fishing and hiking."

"You're just tired from chasing girls, Phil," Naomi snickers.

Holly says, "Especially Ami. You guys have been spending a lot of time together recently. And, Phil, you wouldn't have time to fish even if we had a lake right in front of us. Chasing girls can be a full-time job."

"You're just jealous," says Phil with his grin spread across his face, his body sprawled over a truck tire.

I look over at Holly and can't help but chuckle.

"You're laughing at me, White Boy," she moans.

"Yes, I am. You look cute stuck there in that tire with your head out one side and your bare legs flopping out the other. Actually, Holly, you have kind of nice-looking legs. I guess I hadn't really noticed them before."

"I know you hadn't noticed them before, Jason. That's the problem."

"Problem? What problem? I didn't even know there *was* a problem."

"That's the problem," Naomi laughs from her tire. "You don't understand there's a problem. You're just too lethargic." Both girls seem to think this is hilarious and start laughing hysterically at the same time.

"Never will understand women," I say. "And I spend half my life with them." *Holly really does have nice legs. She looks really good in those cutoffs.*

"Holly, you know what?" I say, but am interrupted by Brad, climbing up our mountain of tires.

"Hey Jason! I've been looking all over for you guys."

"Hi, Brad," says Naomi dreamily. "Grab a tire next to me and relax a while. You deserve it. These mounds of tires are a great place to spend a morning off. Of course, we didn't think any snoopy supervisor would find us here."

"Sorry, don't have time." Brad's out of breath but his eyes are on Naomi. "We've got problems – could be big problems."

"What's up?" I try to stand straight but my rear's still attached to the small tire I was sitting in and I fall back down.

"Cute, White Boy. Real cute. You could just walk around all day with that tire attached to your butt. It would make a great conversation piece."

"Thanks, Holly." I try to pull myself loose by rolling over on my side and dislodging myself from a tire which, from the size of it, could have belonged to the golf cart Naomi was driving around.

"Hey, you guys, get serious. We've got a crisis. Half our workers have just walked off the job. Most of the others are just standing around feeling pissed off."

"What happened?" I ask as I reach for my t-shirt. "What're they mad about?"

"It's the City Council. They had a closed executive session last night and voted five to four to sell all the earthships in an open auction. The radio report said they need cash real bad, so they're selling out."

"They can't do that," Holly screams, jumping out of her tire.

Brad, Philip, and I stand and stare! Then I partially turn away, my face flushed. The other two guys follow suit. Holly, climbing out of her tractor tire, had forgotten to put her blouse back on. I guess she had taken it off while sunbathing in the modesty of her large tire. As I said earlier, males at our community are used to being around girls with no attire at all when we're bathing. But in the last months, I have become more sensitive... or insensitive, or heck – I don't know. Holly's dark, firm breasts gleam with sweat, and I feel more than warm all over.

"Whoops!" Holly's grabbed her blouse and turns around while slipping it on.

"Well, you *did* get my attention," I say, my face still turned away.

"That's good, Jason. I was wondering if I ever would. But I guess I have to take my clothes off to get it though, huh?"

"Um, uh – not really," I mutter, more to myself than to her.

"Well, back to business," Philip says nervously, his mischievous grin sprawled on his face. "I've had my wake-up call for the day."

I pull myself together and ask Brad, "Is this legal? Can the city sell our earthships?"

"I guess so. I'm no lawyer, but we're building on their property... and they never promised us a thing."

Holly turns around, her blouse buttoned and tucked into her shorts. "They can't do this. We won't let them." Her face reminds me of a female bulldog guarding her litter from a pack of rats.

"Well, the shit has already hit the fan, almost literally." Brad continues, looking directly at Naomi as he talks. "Within two hours of the story breaking in this morning's edition of the *L.A. Times*, black city workers hauled two truckloads of human feces from the city sewer plant and dumped it on the steps of the city hall."

"Great idea!" says Philip.

Brad, continues, his voice turning more somber, "The bad news is that during the last hour, rioting's broken out in areas of Compton, Inglewood, and into the San Fernando Valley – around Pacoima."

"Pacoima! Damn, that's where my folks live. I've got to get to a phone and give them a call," Holly says as she bounces from tire to tire, down our little rubber mountain.

"Let's get going," I say, concerned about Holly's family.

The five of us make our way down from the mound of tires and run at a trot, passing through our earthship community on the way back to our compound. As I run, I notice work is entirely stopped on the earthships, but hundreds of people cluster about, talking in small groups. I see Philip slow down and stop, and I do the same. Cliff's sitting off by himself on a stack of tires looking like a monument to our unfinished work, his hands together as if praying, and his head hung low. The expression on his bearded face reflects anxiety and pain. Philip and I look at each other as if asking each other for direction. Philip gives me a weak smile, turns and walks over to Cliff. I follow, yelling to Holly that I'll catch up with her in a couple of minutes.

"Hi, Cliff," says Philip quietly. "Looks like your mind is a million miles away."

"Hello, boys," Cliff answers without his usual humor. Slowly he unfolds his hands and looks up at us, his face tired and drained. "Oh, my mind is here, but my soul is out in the galaxy on vacation somewhere. I see you boys are giving up too. Looks like another victory for the forces of evil and doom."

"We just got the news. What are we to do?" I respond defensively. "Everyone seems to be giving up, going to the camp or their homes. The heart's gone out of everyone, at least for now."

"Oh, you're right, Jason," Cliff says, his head still hung. "The heart has gone out of all of us. But you folks can go back to your community if this project fails. Those of us living here have no place to go – just back to our shacks, the tent cities, or to the streets."

We're all quiet for a minute. I don't know what to say, but Cliff starts in again. "You've all done a great job here. But it's up to us to keep this project going. We can't afford to let it die. In fact, I don't think the nation can afford to let this die. So I ain't giving up." His eyes pick themselves up from the ground and look directly at Phil and me. "I'll be back here, and I won't be alone. You boys mark my words. I'm going to figure out something. We're not done with those bastards from the city."

With that, Cliff stands up, a spark in his eyes, a small grin on his weathered face. He turns and stretches his long arms out, as if he were going to fly, but instead he starts to walk off. He turns back, however, to say, "You boys remember: I'll be back real soon, so don't go too far away." He then turns and slowly heads for the old neighborhood across the street, rubbing his beard as he walks.

After Cliff's gone, Phil and I sigh harmoniously and then continue walking quietly back to camp. Holly's just gotten off the phone and is talking to Luella in front of our tent. "My parents are fine. The rioting is a couple of miles south of them. At least this was a good excuse for me to call them. I've only talked to them twice since I've been back from up north." With that said, she picks up a metal folding chair and sits in rare silence, propping her chin up with the palm of her hand.

Most of our group is back from the earthships. Some of us stand around with our hands in our pockets – bewildered, not knowing what to do. I find a folding chair and set it next to Holly's. I lean dangerously far back, resting my head against a tent post, and ponder our new predicament.

At 8:00 many of our community members gather inside our tent and listen to a radio report. "Violence is once again spreading across the black sections of L.A. and the nation. Even in white, Asian, and Latino communities the unrest is now being acted out by rioting and random acts of violence. Up to this point, the violence – much like in March – has been aimed more at government entities than individuals or particular racial groups. Unfortunately, law enforcement officials expect that to change as the rioting continues."

Officer Jenkens with the L.A. Police Department comes by around 10:00. He tells us they got a tip that a white supremacist group is planning to use this unrest as an opportune time to come in and set fire to what's already built of our new community. An officer received an anonymous phone call at 9:35 stating that the group called The Fourth of July was planning to set fires all over the black sections of L.A., including our new earthship community. Their plan, he thought, was to stir up racial unrest, which would give them the opportunity to gain more support and notoriety.

"I really don't know how tire houses are going to burn," Naomi says. "I don't remember ever seeing one on fire in *our* community."

"I suppose if you put enough gasoline on them, they'd burn real fine," says Derrick, another of our community members.

There's a general consensus that the tire houses will burn if somebody wants that badly enough. That's, however, the only consensus we come to tonight. We talk on into the night, but the dialogue is dispirited.

Before I fall asleep I write my dad a letter about my meeting with my mom and the news about the shutdown. When I'm done I find myself writing an eleven-page letter to my mother and her husband. I try and explain why I'm here and what we're all trying to accomplish. I guess I'm doing a little lobbying, Bill being the mayor's attorney. I'm not sure I'm very articulate, but I do my best... until my eyes just won't stay open any longer.

The next day is no less gloomy. With the rioting going on in the entire city, we're losing much of the police and Army protection we've so far enjoyed. All morning and afternoon we see the soldiers and police loading up and moving out to help protect other areas of the already ravaged city.

At nightfall things are eerily quiet around our camp. It's about midnight, and some of us haven't been able to go to sleep. A half dozen of us decide to stretch our legs – walk through the quietness of our still unoccupied earthship community. As we stroll, I look down the parkway at the earthships all facing south. Without any humans to give them life, they look so desolate.

"I wonder," Holly says bitterly, "if they will last through the night. Either the white supremacists or angry black people will burn them down. I'd better take a good look while we still have the chance. They may not be here in the morning."

"Cheer up. It ain't over 'til it's over," I remind her. "Things will get better if we just hang in there. It's worrying about problems, not the problems themselves, that creates all this stress." Naomi, walking on my other side, looks over at me, closes her eyes, and shakes her head.

As we walk farther, we come to Hayward Avenue, the north part of the perimeter road around the community. Every couple of minutes we see a pair of lights go by in sequences of four or five-minute shifts.

"Those don't look like police cars," Holly says. "More like gang or posse cars – black gang cars. Look! See how they're low to the ground, dark in color, and have red tinted glass all around? They're gang members all right."

"So what's the difference between gang members and posse members?" Brad asks.

"Gangs are like fraternal outlaws, but some have a few social redeeming qualities," Holly says curtly. "Posses are just plain criminals running around in a pack."

Amaranth (or *Ami*, as we call our youngest and most adventuresome member) says, "Well, if these guys are just gang members, let's go over there and find out what's going on."

"No way," Holly tells her. "Your friends here already found out what it's like to deal with posse members. We don't need to push our luck. It's best we just keep as far away as we can from those people."

"Look, you said these guys aren't posse members, and some of them have gotten out of their cars and are talking over there on the corner. I'm going over there and find out what's going on." Without another word, Ami takes off, walking overtly across the street toward the gang members.

"Oh, shit," Holly says. "Here we go again."

"Great," says Philip. "We can't let her go by herself. I'd better go with her." He steps off the curb after Ami. The rest of us, like sheep, blindly follow.

We know we can't catch up with her, and we don't want to run toward the gang members like a herd of stampeding black and white buffalo. So all six of us cautiously walk the two hundred feet to a dimly lit corner to greet five gang members who, according to the back of their black jackets, call themselves the Avengers.

They stand in a loose cluster, casually watching us approach them. I don't feel the expected tightness in my chest. My real intuition is telling me that this is okay, that we're not being threatened.

Ami happily greets The Avengers before the rest of us even get there. "Hey, dudes, what's going on?"

"Not much going down tonight, White Lady," is the reply from a stocky, pony-tailed black man who looks to be in his early twenties. "You white folks out for a stroll this evening?" he asks as he squeezes a little black ball and stares directly at Holly as we walk up next to Ami. Holly, with her thumbs in her jeans pockets, stares back at him, never blinking her eyes.

"As you can obviously see, nigger, I ain't white folk. I'm a Peace Corps volunteer working on places to live so you black asses have somewhere to go when you're done terrorizing the neighborhood."

A smile breaks out across Mr. Pony-tailed Avenger. "Well, Sister —or should I just call you Holly? – you certainly haven't lost any of your spunk, and I am certainly glad someone here's taking care of my black ass. But the reality is, that's why we're here tonight. We don't want any white boys coming over and burning down all your hard work. If anyone's going to burn this place down, it'll be us black brothers and sisters – not some white supremacist group."

"So you guys are guarding our community?" Holly asks, her mouth dangling half open. "That's certainly a switch. You guys get religion or just bored?"

"No, we didn't get religion, and we ain't bored. Like I said," he says, a smile still on his face, "if the city decides to sell these houses to the highest bidder, then we'll burn them down. If they decide to distribute them to the folks who got burned out, then we'll protect them. But we ain't letting no white boys get the first chance at setting the fires.

"So, Black Girl, you and your white friends can go back and sleep in peace, 'cause there ain't no one going to burn Watts tonight. Maybe we'll burn it tomorrow, but it won't burn tonight." He turns his back to us, now facing his stern-looking companions. The conversation's over; we're obviously being dismissed.

We're quick learners... got the message. As we quietly walk back towards our compound, Ami turns back, waves and says, "Good night." Several gang members mutter something that sounds like "Good night" back.

As soon as we're out of hearing distance, I ask Holly, "Why did you talk like that? How did you know that these gang members wouldn't bother us?"

"White Boy, when you live in the jungle, you get to know which animals you can trust and which ones you can't. We were in absolutely no danger back there. Those guys weren't thugs like those punks we met in Compton. Their code of honor wouldn't let them bother us. In fact, they would have defended us with their lives if we were attacked. Like I said, you just gotta know the animals if you're gonna walk in the jungle. By the way," she adds quickly, looking straight ahead as we walk, "I used to know the leader back there. His name is Clyde. We went to high school together."

Holly and I walk the rest of the way back in silence. Holly seems preoccupied and walks in front of the rest of us. Ami and Philip drop behind while talking a mile a minute. Brad and Naomi walk in the middle of our band, chatting quietly. Somehow, this all seems appropriate.

"It's strange," I say to Holly as we arrive at the entrance of our tent and walk inside. "I felt like I knew Clyde back there from someplace before, but I don't know why. How well did you know him in high school?"

"Good night," is Holly's only reply. She walks up to her bunk, pulls herself to the top, climbs in, and doesn't even undress or say a word. She just turns over and looks like she's pretending to be asleep.

*What'd I say? Girls can sure be... moody.* My thoughts then switch back to what's going on around us. *Will the night find violence?* But then I decide it's best not to waste any time thinking about any of it. I don't have any control over how it's going to turn out. I sit on my bed and let my mind go into a quiet meditation until sleep comes.

As I tumble out of my bunk the next morning, I see Holly's still dressed and sitting cross-legged on her bunk, "I heard shots during the night," I say.

"I heard them, too. Don't know what time it was. I was too tired to look. Guess that's the way it'll be from now on. Sorry if I was just a little snippy last night. I was tired I guess."

"No problem. Anything you want to talk about?"

"No, that's okay. It's nothing I can't handle. Anyway," she continues while looking down at her bed, "the black gangs have made peace with one another for the time being. They're probably after white boys now. Actually I don't think anyone knows who they're after. Everyone is just pissed off at everyone else, and no one knows why for sure. It's a crazy world, Jason. It's a very crazy world." With that, she wipes a tear from her cheek.

I try to sound upbeat. "It does seem crazy out there, but feels good with us. I mean the community members and you guys. Like we're one. That's just the way it is at Higher Ground. In one sense, it's like we never left."

"Yeah, I feel the same way." Holly looks up into my eyes. "I've never been to your community, but I think I've been searching for Higher Ground my whole life. I do feel the love between us all these last several months and, White Boy, I do have to admit I like it. I like it a lot. I just don't want it to change, okay? Jason, even if things get worse and you find out some things about me you don't like, promise me you won't let it change what is between us? Promise?"

"Okay, sure." That's all I think to say.

She climbs down off her bunk and we hug each other for a long time. The warmth of holding Holly is like nothing I have experienced before. Even though she seems sad, her body seems so firm and alive. I feel a stirring again through my entire being. I know we've made a connection that will go on with me forever. Holly's cheeks are wet against mine, and I can taste the salt in my mouth as tears run down our cheeks. As I hold her, I glance across at Naomi who has just awakened and is propped up on her elbow. Her lopsided grin stretches from ear to ear. Not saying a word, she just keeps grinning.

"I guess we'd better get to breakfast," I stammer, my heart beating fast, my head in confusion. Holly's arms drop from my back and mine from hers. Our eyes lock for several seconds, and then we move apart to get ready for the day.

What to do? This is the question on everyone's mind at breakfast this morning. As we watch the sun rise in the east, we see wispy streams of smoke in the air. The smoke is from fires still burning from the night before.

"At least," Philip says, "the smoke is only in wisps, and it isn't coming from our earthships."

"That's the good news," says Brad. "The bad news is that the Army cooks told me this morning that the rest of their company is pulling out today. They don't know where they're going or when they're coming back. So, I guess we're on our own."

Our community calls a meeting after breakfast. We know other communities are doing the same. After hearing from Brad about the Army pulling out, we're all a little more disheartened. The question is: Should we continue work on the earthship community, or is it time to go home to our own communities? Opinions are as diverse as the people are, but the common denominator is no one knows for sure what we should do. We sit in our folding chairs in a circle outside our tent. So much seems out of our hands at this point.

"I don't want to sound like a naysayer," says Sam, a quiet, middle-aged man from our community. "But I am not sure if we're doing much good here. We started off like gang busters, but now it seems like no one cares. Personally, I miss my family. Maybe it's time we call it a day, go back home and let the smoke clear."

"I care," says Luella as she stands up and looks around the group with a sober face. "I realize it's hard on many you, being away from your families and friends, and I can't blame anyone for leaving. But I just want everyone to know I do appreciate every one of you and what you've done. My life will never be the same because of the love you've shown me."

After she sits down there are several minutes of silence. I remember what Cliff said, that he wasn't giving up, that he would be back, and that he wouldn't be alone. Philip and I look at each other across the circle. He looks serious as he nods his head, and I take his cue to stand up. I look around our group at new friends and old. My eyes rest briefly on Luella, who has sat back down. She gives me a quick but friendly smile back.

My voice is a little shaky, and my throat is dry, but I am certain of what I want to say. "I know everyone is discouraged. I certainly am too, but I strongly believe that we can't give up. We knew all along that it was going to be difficult. I think we all know how politicians change their minds when they feel the winds of change in the air. I'm sure before too long the pressure from the people will prevail, and the politicians will come up with a much better plan. I, for one, don't want to leave my new friends here with the job only half completed. I think we need to stay and wait for that to happen." I briefly look directly in Holly's eyes. Then I sit down, and another several minutes of silence follow.

Then Marv stands up, looks around the room, and starts speaking. "It seems like on this trip our younger people have grown either wiser or more brash. Whatever it is, I like it. I believe the leadership and the drive they've shown has gotten us to where we are today in building this new community, and I believe it is what we continue to need. I think we must wait as Jason advised. Let's keep our faith. If we hold the love, love will prevail." Marv sits back down.

There is quiet again. I look around the room at our other community members. I can see everyone in the room is giving much thought to what's been said. We have learned from years of experience that important decisions often require each individual to take time and contemplate his own feelings about what is happening.

Finally, Irene looks around the room and breaks the silence by asking everyone if they're ready to vote. "I have a simple suggestion from Jason and Marv that we should sit tight and wait for a couple of weeks while things get ironed out with the city. Does anyone else have anything they want to add or make any other motions?" Irene looks around the room again, this time taking her time and focusing on each person several seconds before moving on to the next. "Okay, let's get started. Would everyone please raise his hand and indicate by the number of fingers where you stand on this issue? Remember, five fingers means you're in total agreement; four means you support the motion; three means you can live with it but you're not excited about the idea; two means you don't like the idea and want more discussion; and one means you're totally against it and you'll subvert it."

It takes Irene less than five minutes to look around the room and get everyone's vote. "So we've got 20 fives, 5 fours, and 2 threes from our original community members; and 11 fives from our new friends. So, it looks like we're staying," says Irene with a broad smile.

# Chapter 11

"Everyone get off their beds and away from their beds!"
I hear a female voice yell and it sounds like Luella. "Get away
from your steel lockers, they could fall! Hurry up get in the
middle of the room."

*What is going on?* I think to myself. *Is this the end of the
world?*

Crash – God that was my locker. "I can't even stand up!"
I yell as I drop to the floor on all fours.

"Jason are you OK? Naomi's voice screams as she grabs
my hand. "What is happening? I can't see a thing."

"It's an earthquake," yells Luella from somewhere left of
us. "Now get in the middle of the tent and get down on your
knees and protect your neck. It will be over in a minute, I
hope." Crash – another locker hits the floor and we can hear
its contents pour out on to the floor.

"Is that you Jason?" says Marv in a whisper.

"It's me Marv. Are you all right?"

"I fell out of bed. I hurt my back but I'm all right."

"Everyone," shouts Luella again, "get in the middle of
the tent, away from anything that can fall on you. Is anyone
else hurt?"

"I think every one else is OK," Brad answers.

"Here – I found my flashlight," says Naomi as she hands
it to Luella.

"The shaking is slowing down," says Brad as he crawls over next to me and Naomi.

"Where's Holly?" I ask. "Has anyone seen her? Holly!" I yell, "Holly,"– but no answer.

"Is everybody else in the tent accounted for?" asks Luella, as we all huddle in the middle of the tent.

"I think we're all here," I say as Luella shines the light around. Everybody but Holly. "Has any one seen her?" Nobody says a word.

"We've got two flashlights now," says Luella, "and the shaking has stopped. Marv you stay put. The rest of us, let's search, and hurry, she could be unconscious under one of the lockers."

Minutes go by as we look through strewn around beds and lockers. There's a couple of medium aftershocks as we search, but no sign of Holly. I have this lump forming in the bottom of my stomach. We all meet again in the middle of the tent.

"Shit! Where could she be?" exclaims Luella, "she just couldn't have disappeared."

"Everyone quiet please," says Jess, let's do a two minute quiet time and ask for intuitive guidance."

We're all silent, the only noise is people shouting in the distance away from our tent. The silence is eerie but I almost laugh as somebody starts snoring close by.

"Wait a minute!" says Jess as he stands up and walks with the flashlight over to where Holly's bunk is still standing upright.

"I'll be darned," he says as he picks up the end of her blanket and we all walk over and stare in disbelief. There is Holly under her covers, curled up in a ball at the end of her bed, still sound asleep.

"Mm Mm – what do you guys have that flashlight in my face for?" she says as she struggles to open her eyes. "It's still dark, how come you're all up? Who made the mess?"

After finding Holly still sound asleep in her bed, the mood is momentarily more lighthearted.

"Look guys, it's only because I'm such an enlightened trusting being that I could sleep through that heavy of an earthquake. I think you guys need to start giving me more respect," Holly laments. We all laugh and I look at Holly and shake my head.

"This reminds me of nights back home in the community when bunches of us teenagers would stay up all night," says Naomi. "It was fun but I can remember when we were younger, maybe seven or eight, and it wasn't so much fun. The community was only several years old. Us kids would get together and talk about Higher Ground and whether it would survive. We wondered if the people outside, who weren't a part would come in and get us because we had a different lifestyle than theirs. Most of us had seen TV and movies before we came. We were too little to realize that most of the violence we had been watching was just producers and advertisers selling their souls in the name of giving people more fear and excitement. We were so young we just didn't know the difference.

"Fortunately our parents or elders, like Marv here would come in and explain that there was nothing to fear – as long as we kept putting out love, that's what we would get back. It took us a while to get it. But that whole experience brought us much closer together. Those nights taught us how to bond in a way I never knew existed before."

"It's different in Watts in some ways, though the same in others," replies Luella. "When we were little we would have slumber parties and even living in Watts the main source of violence we were exposed to was the TV. The gangs never bothered families, and, in fact, that's what I think the gangs are, just a more dysfunctional version of extended families. If those members grew up in communities like yours, they wouldn't need a gang to be in.

"But you know as you get older it changes, and then you've got to deal with all the drug dealers and posses in school and on the street. Sometimes when I was in high school, us girls would get together and talk about boys and such. But then we would start philosophizing and wonder why things had to be the way they were. It's always seemed so strange living in a country where millions of people are living in what I'd call mansions, while the majority of us black people are still living in slums that aren't hardly fit for humans.

"I always wonder what goes on in those wealthier people's mind, how they can live in those big houses when they know there's people who can hardly afford a roof over their head. Shit, my ex-sister-in-law and her six-year-old daughter moved in with four other homeless women in a broken down school bus. She works at McDonald's for $6.50 an hour. Her total take-home wouldn't even make car payments for many people."

"Amen sister, we all have friends and relatives like that," interjects Bennie.

"Then it often seems like those wealthier are the same people who get up in arms any time somebody would want to raise the minimum wage. They're already giving President Mandell shit for her proposals. Just doesn't make any sense to me," continues Luella, sounding more confused and hurt than angry.

"I can't even imagine what it must have been like before the fires," interjects Brad. "I feel like my life has been so sheltered compared to yours. But I do know we're going to change it – dammit, it's going to change. It will never be like that here again."

"Man," says Benny as he strums his guitar, "you don't even know the half of it. I am ready to sign up and go back to Oregon with you honkies. Where we're sitting right now was big time posse territory and you'd have been dead white meat if you'd been sitting on the corner a year ago. This place was like a battle zone. I heard you guys don't have any fast food places at your communities so you white dudes may have never heard of Taco Bell. It's a Mexican joint and there used to be one near where the mess tent is. Anyway that place over the last sixteen years had fifty-eight drive by shootings. From what I hear it's a record for fast food joints nationwide, though I've never heard them bragging about it on TV.

"But I'm with you, brother we are going to change it – I am with you white folks – we ain't going back."

"No way," agrees Holly, "we're never going back."

"No way," says Luella, "we're done with that crap. This is our community and I am with you white people on this one. It'll turn around, I can feel it."

With that Benny picks up the beat with his guitar. The aftershocks continue hour after hour and we remain curled up in blankets sprawled across the middle of our tent floor with several large candles in the middle, spending the rest of the night rolling with the quakes and singing gospel to bolster our spirits.

"Hey everybody, we're alive!" says Philip as he walks through the front tent flap at 6 a.m. "You people sure are lousy housekeepers though, look at this place. You should be ashamed!"

"You're lucky I am too tired to throw my pillow," responds Naomi as most of us lay around exhausted, while others sleep scattered across the floor.

"But by the grace of God I want you to know there is not a crack in any one of those earthships out there. Brian and I just made the tour and they look perfect, but unfortunately the radio is saying there's been millions of dollars' damage to the surrounding communities. But these earthship homes are earthquake-proof, at least to 7.6 on the Richter Scale. Now all we gotta do is get back to work and finish this job!"

Pro football is like
nuclear warfare—
there are no winners,
only survivors.

Frank Gifford

# Chapter 12

"This is Josh Richardson for KWTV in Los Angeles, California. It's Monday, June 2, 2012. This is my five-minute personal commentary on the news of L.A., the nation, and around the world.

"The United States of America is in chaos. Widespread rioting across the country is now the norm. Burning and pillaging is ongoing in every major city in the United States. The police, National Guard, and Army are trying to keep a lid on the unrest, but to little or no avail. As has been the case with all the last year's unrest, the real issue doesn't seem to be Watts, the city of L.A., poverty, the federal government, or anything we can put our finger on. People are frightened, frustrated, and angry. Most of those I have interviewed don't even know why.

"We are used to blaming other people: politicians, lawyers, bankers, or whomever; but the questions and fears in people's minds go much deeper. The 'buy-more, have-more' feeling of the 20th Century seems to have gone. The long-term gnawing inside people is boiling to the surface, as if large boils which have festered and festered are now finally breaking out all at once. The rioting and unrest spreading across the country is like pus spreading across the skin when the boil breaks. It is messy and unsightly – but only on the surface. The deeper question is: When the pus is wiped away, will the wounds heal or become more infected and spread throughout the body... until death?

"People have lost confidence, or should I say faith, in their government, their peers, themselves, and the new consumer technology complex that dominates our life. More importantly, many have lost their belief in the presence of a power higher than mankind. Even though religious attendance itself has been growing at a steady pace since the troubled times of the turn of the century, the connection between religion and a higher power have seemingly been severed. Religion has become a separate entity in itself, apart from the mystical, mysterious powers of faith and spirituality.

"The dogma of many religions has become more and more peppered with what we should be fearing instead of what we should be loving. Fear has become a way of life for most of the inhabitants of planet Earth; fear now runs rampant and unleashed throughout America.

"We need a fundamental change in the way we are living, but what is that going to be? As the President warned in her speech in Watts over a month ago, 'Is this the disintegration or the collapse of our nation as we know it?' I wish I had the answer. I simply don't know, but I believe we're going to have to give the President a chance and pass her Ten-Point Plan. I urge the House and the Senate to pass it immediately, and get it on the President's desk within the week.

"I ask every one of you listeners who agree with me to call or write your congressman and senators today; urge them to pass the President's proposal as she has written it. I also ask you to call or fax the Los Angeles City Council to reverse their decision to sell to the highest bidder the emerging community being built in Watts. This is a flagrant misuse of a wonderful project that the President herself inspired.

"We all have ahead of us a Herculean task – one designed more for gods and goddesses than mere mortals like ourselves. As the President said, we have no other choice.

"I thank you and good night. This is Josh Richardson, until tomorrow."

"It's all happening just like the President said it would," Jess says quietly. "We're either going to head in a new direction or perish. Do the rest of you mind if I change the channel and see what else is on? This guy was good, but I've seen enough news this week to last me a lifetime."

There are about fourteen of us watching an antique T.V. that Cliff gave us after the quake. Several of us encourage Jess to change the channel. He tries half a dozen channels, but they're all more news programs or documentaries on acts of violence and mayhem.

"That's all there is on T.V. now," Holly says in disgust. "Show after show of the most grisly, bone-chilling murders, rapes, or any type of graphic violence that people will watch. That's what America is watching. It's sick!"

"No wonder the world has gone mad," Jess says. "The violence tolerance level's gotten so high that now anything is considered normal. It's crazy. The earthquake wasn't half as bad as this stuff."

Philip rises from his chair, walks over, turns off the T.V., then reaches behind it and unplugs the cord. We all applaud, and Philip bows. I can feel the mood lighten. We're getting nervous, but we're still together.

We've all gotten very restless. A group of the local people have challenged representatives from Higher Ground to a soccer match. It's an interesting challenge. We do play soccer at the community, but we've always played it intermurally and never had set teams – always concentrated more on group participation than winning. I feel we might be out of our league, but Philip tells me not to worry.

I'm not the only one with doubts. "They're all men," Holly whines as we watch our opponents warm up. "You guys won't have a chance... not with me on your team."

"What do you mean 'you guys'?" asks Naomi, hands on her hips and staring into Holly's face. "We're all in this together, and you're going to be right out there with us."

"But I'm uncoordinated," Holly says. "I mean, I like soccer, but I wasn't good enough for my high school team and that always bummed me out. I was encouraged to play when I was little. Then when I got to be sixteen they said I wasn't good enough anymore – that we had to have a winning team at Grant High to be cool. I was also told I wasn't cool enough to be a cheerleader – guess that's when my school life started going downhill. Like I said you guys won't have a chance with me on your team."

"It doesn't matter," Brad says. "We just play for fun; it doesn't matter who wins."

"But Brad, look at their fancy blue and white uniforms, like professionals. Guys around here take sports really seriously. It's like all some of them live for. Though I bet most of them probably spend more of their time with a beer in their hand watching it on T.V. than actually participating. But I gotta say: these guys look for real."

"Enough excuses. Come on, Holly," Naomi says as she drags Holly by the elbow out onto the field.

Somebody blows a whistle. We're about to start in one of the old parks that was here before the fire. We've managed to get the grass greened up enough to be usable, and we've got a rough field marked out. There's ten of us: six guys, four girls. The other team's agreed to play with ten also, even though they have twelve players altogether.

We do look a little disorganized and, as the game gets going, it becomes apparent that they *are* in a different class than us. Five to nothing at the half, and I think they're being nice.

"I told you guys." Holly says as we sit in a circle sipping our water. "If you didn't have me, the game would be closer."

"No way," says Brian. "You played well, Holly. They're just a better team, that's all."

"Yea, Holly!" "We love playing with you." "You're a kick!" the others chime in.

"Well, this *is* fun, but you guys really don't care if we're losing?" Holly asks.

"No," says Brad. "We've played our best. Like Brian said, they're better prepared but I am having a blast. We're going to hold them to three points in the second half, and that will be a moral victory."

"Don't take it so seriously, Holly," says Ami, our best player. "This whole thing of taking sports so seriously in our culture is a bunch of crap. Everyone's always trying to be better than everyone else so they can feel better about themselves. It's insane. In our community we're about *all* of us having good self-esteem and not just the few that excel at sports."

"Come on, you guys," says Ami as she jumps up. "Let's warm up, dance and have some fun." We find ourselves in a train, holding the waist of the person in front as we dance around the field.

"Seven to two. Not bad," laughs Holly. "That was a ball. I just can't believe the way you scored that last goal, Ami. You just flew down the field like a gust of wind. You're so graceful."

"Boy, were those guys surprised!" says Phil, as we all walk off the field with our arms wrapped around one another.

It's five days later, and the rioting is still going on. We are all sitting around our tent playing cards when Holly starts complaining. "White Boy, all this smoke in the air must be polluting my lungs. After nineteen years in L.A., you'd think my lungs would be used to anything by now, but it's getting worse."

"I think you need to see a doctor other than our community doctor, Holly," Naomi says. "Ours deal primarily in preventive medicine, but you've been coughing for three weeks now. We need to get you to a specialist. You know what Dr. Ron said about the spread of TB and that new stuff: Bacterial Bacteriophage. These viruses have become immune to antibiotics. Because of their immunity, these viruses can just wear you down to nothing if you don't take care of yourself."

"Thanks, Naomi. That makes me feel real good," Holly says between coughs.

"I've been worried about you, and Nate also," I say as I walk over and put my hand on Holly's forehead. "He's been coughing too. And you guys were working together for a long time up north. I think we need to get both of you checked out."

"I don't have any health insurance, and I'm sure Nate doesn't either." Holly takes my hand away from her forehead and sticks her tongue out at me. "Besides, all the hospitals are full. Between diseases and injuries from the rioting, there just isn't any room left. I'll be okay; I'm sure it's just a summer cold. I just need to get a good night's sleep tonight. As long as no one throws any rats on me, and I can sleep through earthquakes. I'm gonna turn in now," she says as she gets up, walks by me, and sticks her tongue out again. "Good night, everybody."

As the rest of us sit here, I notice the smoke has gotten worse; it engulfs us much of the time. According to the news report, every night new buildings are set on fire. The reporter last night said that a dozen fires were set in the Hollywood Hills dividing Los Angeles and the Valley. Over 2,000 acres have burned, and the fires are still spreading.

We have several naturopathic doctors with us, including Dr. Ron and Dr. Speigle from Higher Ground. They held a community meeting this morning after several members started complaining about prolonged, severe sore throats and coughing spells. Although they've never dealt with

Bacterial Bacteriophage before, they checked out several of our members, including Holly. Besides their throats being red and inflamed, the doctors couldn't find anything wrong.

With all the smoke, it's tough to know what's going on and what to do next. I think many of us are starting to suffer from depression.

It's Saturday morning, and we've been shut down two weeks now. I'm really worried about Holly and our other sick members. Holly's been lying around a lot, and her cough has gotten worse. She's starting to call me Jason instead of White Boy. The energy has all drained out of her, and she's very mellow and peaceful. It's so unlike her. It worries all of us – me, in particular.

Holly lies in her top bunk, and I am in mine. She peers over at me and quietly asks, "Jason, tell me about yourself, what you like, what you don't like. You don't seem addicted to sports like so many men. What do you do for fun? You've never really talked much about you. You usually just talk about your community."

"Well, there's not a whole lot to tell about me that you don't already know. I try to live a balanced life. I have my practice, eat right, do Tai Chi, paint, swim and meditate. I do all these thing all week long. I also play sports – tennis, soccer, handball; I cross-country ski. We play a lot of sports at Higher Ground, but we try to play for fun, not real competitively. As you saw, I'm not a great soccer player, but I like to play. Playing tennis, hiking, making ceramics, and fly-fishing in our ponds and streams are my favorite things to do."

"Don't you guys have a football team or a baseball team?"

"No. We encourage sports. We do play softball, but we don't play football. Football always seemed rather violent. I guess we're more into the kind of sports where everyone can play more equally, so no one ends up giving up and becoming a couch potato, or feels bad because they're not good enough."

I was reading in *Newsweek* last month..." Luella pipes up and smiles apologetically. "Sorry to interrupt, but I couldn't help but overhear you two. Anyway, T.P. Elliot was saying that if we go to college, it's even worse than high school because the college recruits mercenary players from all over the world just so they can say they have a winning team. The average players, or even the better ones, usually have little or no chance at playing for their own school.

"What bugs me is that coaches put out all this bull that teamwork is what's important, yet everyone – even the coaches – worships the hero, the star. The hero doesn't have to treat people nicely or be a good person, but if he can hit the ball farther than anyone else and win games, that's all that matters. It's a crock."

"Yeah, I believe what you guys are saying. I've just tried not to think about it," says Holly, jumping to her knees, some of her old excitement coming back. "You know, most of us girls used to feel bad about ourselves because we didn't have a perfect body or a gorgeous face. But damn it! Now we get it from all directions. If we don't have a great body, if we don't make the first team, or if we're not good enough to be a star at something – we're in deep shit. Right?"

"Unfortunately, you're right," Luella says and I nod with her in agreement.

"I can remember my boyfriend Clyde in high school, how political he found the football team. He felt he was driven to quit because he didn't fit in. He felt so bad because he couldn't wear a letterman's jacket. I think that's why he and a lot of the other guys and girls joined the gangs and posses – they didn't fit in, so they had to belong to something else.

"But Jason, you did it again. Every time I talk or ask about you, you turn it around to your community or problems outside community. Come on. I love hearing about your community, but I really care about you. Get a life, Jason. Think about yourself once in a while. Are all white boys as intellectual as you? Don't you ever get emotional?"

"I get emotional, Holly. I guess I've just never been very good at talking about myself."

"Well, you need to learn, Jason. You guys are humble personally, but not when it comes to talking about your community. There it all sounds so perfect. Don't you ever feel sad or depressed?"

"I feel sad now, Holly. I feel sad that you're sick, and I don't know what's wrong. I feel sad you won't go to the hospital. Actually, I guess I don't feel sad you won't go to the hospital – I feel mad. It's really frustrating to care about someone so much, and they won't even go find out what's wrong."

"Excuse me," says Luella, "but I'm outta here. This is getting a little too personal for me. See you guys at lunch. Bye."

"Bye, Luella," Holly says. Then she turns to me without missing a beat. "So, Jason..." She lies back down, props herself up on her elbow and stares at me intently. "So... how much do you care about me?"

I hesitate, nervously playing with my pillow. "Oh, I care a lot. You know that." I notice she has ignored my comments about her going to the hospital.

"No, Jason. I don't know how much you care. Do you care about me in the same way that you care about Naomi? A good friend? Or is there something more?" She looks me straight in the eye, her voice sounding so serious.

"Um, well, I guess I care more, Holly." I feel the perspiration under my arms and on my hands. "I guess I feel differently. I've never felt so close to anyone before. I mean, you're on my mind all the time. I've never tried to put it in words – even in my head."

"Like a girlfriend, Jason? Do you think of me like a girlfriend? Or just a friend?" Holly slides her bare legs over the side of the bed and stares at me even more intently.

"Um, like a girlfriend. I've never had a real serious girlfriend before, but I do think of you as a girlfriend, not just a friend," I sneak my sweaty hands under my blanket, trying to dry them off with my covers.

"Good, Jason. You're doing better. How about me being a black girl. What do you think of that?"

"Well, I guess I never thought much about it at all. You just seem like a person to me – a really special person, actually a really beautiful, lovely special person. But I never thought of you as black, white, or anything else."

"You're doing much better, Jason, much better. You're actually showing some emotion. I actually heard your voice crack, and you definitely are turning beet red."

I put my hand to my cheek, and it does feel warm; in fact, my whole body feels like it's in a sweat. I can feel myself getting really nervous. "Well, I guess I'd better go," I stammer, feeling like I really need to get some fresh air. "I was going to walk out to the earthships and see how they're doing. Okay? You take it easy. Don't get up. I'll see you at lunch. Bye."

I'm already dressed, so I jump off my bed and head for the door. As I reach the door of the tent, I turn. Holly is still sitting on her bed, a half frown on her face.

"Good-bye, Jason," is all she says, and then her frown turns to a sly grin, accompanied by a wink.

*Wow*, I think as I walk in the fresh air towards the earthship. *In love! In love with Holly. That's good,* I think. *Real good.* I actually find myself practically skipping by the time I arrive at our first earthship.

It is a rather strange sight. As far as the eye can see: empty earthships in every direction. Someone not familiar with an earthship would notice they are certainly different-looking than conventional American houses. Most of them are thirty by sixty feet. The front of the earthship is either very long or wide, with panes of glass comprising most of it, like a long window with wooden slats between the panes. Behind the panes is a six-foot greenhouse area with black tile floors designed to collect and store the heat until it is needed. The outer wall in the back and on the sides is rounded adobe about twelve-feet high. The roof is flat with a slight pitch to keep the water running into culverts that take it to a cistern underneath the house. That's where the water is stored for future bathroom and greenhouse use. I've heard the neighborhood people call them futuristic-looking; to me, they're just everyday houses.

I open the door and walk into the earthship nearest to where I stand. It feels cool and inviting inside. We hadn't thought of putting locks on the doors; we never use locks back home. I assume whoever moves into the home can decide if they want to install them.

The inside of the earthship is empty, but a warm feeling prevails, not unlike what I imagine going back to the womb would be. The inside adobe walls are sand-colored. The windows in front and the skylights give a light airy feeling, while the heavy thick outer wall gives a real feeling of security. There are a few inside walls in an earthship – around the bathroom and the bedrooms. The idea is to let the light from the south-facing window stretch all the way to the back of the house. I've lived most of my life in an earthship, and a feeling of nostalgia sweeps through my entire body. I've been gone from home several months now, but it seems like years.

I walk back outside into the 90-degree heat and head to where the latest earthships are being built. As I walk around the corner, much to my surprise, I see Brad, Philip and eight other community members, along with Cliff and other neighbors from the surrounding area. They're pounding tires and pouring sand, working steadily... if not overly enthusiastically.

"I didn't know anyone was still working," I say in amazement to no one in particular as I walk up to the small group.

"We just started this morning," Brad says as he stops working. We give each other a big hug. "We were tired of sitting on our butts all day, so we figured we might as well be out here working instead of staying in our tents complaining."

"We've been waiting for you, White Boy," Cliff says, his old smile back on his face. "So what do you think? Did you come to work or to talk?"

"To work," I say with a laugh and a shrug of my shoulders. "Where do you want me to start?"

Cliff hands me a shovel and, with a grin, points to a pile of crushed concrete that needs to be loaded into several stacked tires.

Philip, with his normal acre-wide grin, says, "I came to the tent to tell you we were going to work this morning. But you looked very *busy*. I didn't want to interrupt anything." We both laugh.

We work until 6:00 and then stack up our tools. I'm dirty and tired as we head back to our tents.

"Where's Holly?" I ask no one in particular as I walk into our tent and give a cursory glance around.

"Naomi took her and Nate over to the hospital," Jess volunteers as he walks up and puts his hand on my shoulder. "Holly was coughing a lot more, and so was Nate. You know Naomi. She couldn't find anything to drive around here, so she went over to the Army compound. She, Ami, and Luella somehow jerryrigged the only bus those Army boys left behind. Then she just drove it up to the tent door and told Holly and Nate to get in or else. Not exactly sure what the 'or else' was, but it worked. They headed down the road in a clamor of grinding gears and turned the wrong way when they got to the first stop sign. But we all know Naomi; they'll make it just fine. Naomi wanted us to tell you not to worry, Jason. They'll be back sometime tonight."

*Not to worry? Not to fear? Nothing to fear?* I've learned all my life not to fear, but here it is again. Ever since I left Higher Ground, fear just hangs around the edges, waiting to creep in if I let down my guard.

"Thanks, Jess." I go and walk over to our mess hall. Since the Army's gone, community members have taken over the cooking duties. I must say, the quality of the food has gotten even better. I sit down at a table by myself with a salad, bowl of spaghetti, and a quarter loaf of French wheat bread, but I have lost my appetite. I take a few bites, but end up taking my full plate of food with me to my tent. Maybe I'll be hungry later.

I few hours ago I realized I was actually romantically in love and on cloud nine. Now I'm just plain worried. I put my food down on my locker, lie down on my bunk and wait.

"Hey, Jason," Philip says as he walks up to my bunk and puts his chin on the edge of my mattress. "Want to play some cards? We've got a game going up front."

"No, thanks. I think I'll just lie here and mope."

"Oh great, Jason," Philip says with a smirk. "That's gonna really help. Everything's going to be just fine. But I understand where you're at. If you need somebody to talk to, just give me a yell."

Philip turns and walks back to the sitting area in front of the tent and goes back to playing cards with Brian. I roll over onto my stomach, put my pillow over my eyes, and ponder my situation. But my eyes are too heavy and I start to dream.

*Holly and I are hiking hand in hand through the meadow, past the fish-rearing ponds that skirt our forest reserve. We're on our way back from our hundred-acre community garden and carry a sack of lettuce and beets for our dinner tonight at my father's home. We stroll down into our parkway where our apple and pear trees are blossoming out in pink and white-colored umbrellas. The wildflowers between the trees have just popped out in a maze of red, pink, and blue. We walk by one of our childcare centers, and children are everywhere on this warm spring day.*

*"Hi, Jason!" "Hi, Jason!" Kalie, Pasha, and Gillian scream in harmony as they run up to me and throw their arms around my legs and dance around Holly and me.*

*"Who's your girlfriend?" asks dark-haired little six-year-old Kalie as she drags a laughing Holly over to a group of tables set up under a bright maroon awning.*

*Liz, who works in the childcare center, comes over with her perpetual smile and hands giggling Kalie a vase off the back of the table. Kalie pats the vase several times and hands it to Holly. "I made this vase yesterday, and it just came out of the kiln this morning; it's a gift to you."*

*"For me?" stammers Holly as she kneels down and examines the small gold vase.*

*"Yep, it's for you. See the angel on the side? She's really real. It's her job to make sure you always find your way back to Higher Ground, no matter what happens to you. Don't ever forget that."*

*"I don't know what to say, but thank you so much. It's so pretty." Then Holly reaches to her ears, undoes her earrings and hands them carefully to Kalie. "My sister made these for me, and they are very special to me. So special that I want you to have them."*

*"They're beautiful. They have angels too, and they look just like wind chimes..."*

"Hey, Jason, wake up. Wake up!" I roll over and Naomi's face is right in mine.

"Naomi! What time is it?" I was just dreaming that I was back at the community with Holly. Are you back from the hospital?"

"It's past midnight, Jason," Naomi puts her hand gently on my shoulder. "Holly, Nate and I are back from the hospital. We finally got in... after waiting four hours in line.

What a mess! That hospital is total chaos. You get in line just to get in another line."

"I don't care about the hospital," I nearly shout. "I just want to know what you guys found out. What's wrong with Holly and Nate?"

"We don't know anything yet," Holly says very quietly as she walks up next to Naomi. Boy, I'm relieved to see her. "They took tests, lots of tests. Won't know anything for two or three days. The doctor told us to separate anyone who's been coughing into another tent."

Nate speaks up as he takes his clothes out of his locker and puts them in his old gray bag. "If it's TB, that's very contagious. We'll grab our things and start moving."

"Separate us?" *Is this a bad dream?* Holly looks at me as if in a trance, turns away, and walks over to the others who, like her, have been coughing. They've gathered in a group, waiting to hear what she found out. She explains the situation and they begin to pack their bags to leave.

I jump down from my bunk, not sure what to do. "Can I help you pack, Holly? Is there anything I can do?"

"Jason, there's nothing you can do right now, answers Holly in a very controlled voice. "I'm done packing. I'll be fine. Just don't get too close to me!" She puts out her arm to block me. "I don't want you getting some horrible disease, like I have." She grabs my hand though, and gives it a squeeze. Her smile quickly disappears as she picks up her old duffel bag and walks out of the tent door. I watch as her and Nate walk to an empty tent near the end of our row... and disappear inside.

I go past Philip and Brian, who are standing with their hands in their pockets by our tent door, go to my bunk and climb in.

"You all right?" Philip hollers.

"I'm fine. Thanks again, Phil. See you in the morning."

This is becoming one of the longest nights of my life. I toss and turn the whole night. I keep waking from a recurring nightmare of Holly being carried off by gang members as I stand by helplessly. I am more than glad to finally see the sun peeking into my tent, announcing the morning.

I look over but don't see Holly's smiling face. As I climb out of bed, I notice Naomi's already gone. Her bed is made tight, and she is nowhere to be seen. I immediately head down to the tent where Holly and the others are staying. It's identical to our tent except on the outside is a large white sign with black letters: *Quarantine. No Admittance.*

When he sees my head poking through the flap, Dr. Speigle comes over to the door of the tent. "Hi, Jason," he says with an empathetic smile. "Sorry, you can't come in right now. We're trying to take all the precautions we can. We should have some surgical masks here by this evening. If you and Holly each wear one, you should be safe. You did come to see Holly, didn't you?"

"Yes sir, I did."

*Safe.* That's the last word I want to hear. I just want to see Holly. I leave the quarantine tent and start slowly walking with my hands in my pockets towards our earthships. As I get closer, I notice that there is a much larger group starting work today. There must be close to 300 workers preparing to work on half a dozen unfinished earthships.

"Well," I say to Brad as I walk up and find him and Philip unloading a bathtub from a pickup truck. "Looks like we're back in business."

"I think so," Brad says as they set the tub on the ground. "The city just announced a new plan this morning. We were listening to them on the morning news. I guess the Mayor's attorneys did a reversal and advised the Council that selling to the highest bidder could damage them both politically and legally.

"They're going to give the Watts-Compton area the status of a new, separate city. They said the people in it could call it Los Miracles or anything they want. Also, the City Council is going to hold a lottery in three weeks. Anyone who lost a home in the fire is eligible to get an earthship. It will cost them just $25,000, payable over ten years. That's what the city figures it will have invested in the lots and the material to finish each earthship."

Philip, who's been helping Jeff unload the bathtub, says, "The commentator said he also thought President Mandell must have put some pressure on the city fathers to come up with this new plan. He said the federal government would probably give L.A. a loan to cover the amount of the lots until they get paid back from the people who win them. I knew the President would do something," he adds with a grin.

"Finally, some good – and interesting – news. We can sure use some." I think, *I'll have to call my mother. Maybe Bill has a bigger heart than I thought.* "So what do you guys think's going to happen? Will the people come back to work? Will the rioting and looting stop?"

"Don't have a clue," Brad says with a frown. "Except for Cliff and his friends, no one's come to help who doesn't belong to our community or Habitat for Humanity. The news commentator didn't seem to think the rioting was going to stop. He said Congress is still in an uproar. They haven't passed Mandell's Ten-Point Plan. Each congressman seems to have his or her own agenda. The President said she's going to take it to the people in a referendum. Until something happens, I guess the rioting and unrest will continue. The City Council's action may take a little steam out of the unrest, at least here locally."

"Well, at least we're back to work. I need something to do to take my mind off Holly and the others who are sick. So let's get to work. Tell me where you want me."

Brad says, "You can help Philip and me unload these bathtubs, and then you can help us figure out how to install them. We're not plumbers by any stretch of the imagination."

By late afternoon we have over a thousand workers back on the job. Most of the members from other communities make the decision to stay and wait, the same as us; however, Habitat for Humanity lost about half of its people. Many of those coming in this afternoon are people who were burned out in the fires and live in the tent city. Several city workers bring in backhoes, a front-end loader, and some badly needed construction material, with the promise of much more by the end of the week.

As I work, I keep thinking, *Where's Naomi? It's not like her to be out here working if everyone else is.* I know she'll show up eventually and that she can take care of herself, but it seems strange to be without Holly and Naomi both. I'm glad to have Philip and Brad to work with, and I feel a little silly for missing the girls so much.

We quit work at quarter to six so we can get back to watch the 6:00 news. Rioting's going on in Washington, D.C. Things look bad. Mobs are attempting to storm the Capitol Building where Congress is in session trying to make a decision on the President's plan. So far, police and regular Army troops in full riot gear have kept rioters out of the building, but things look almost desperate. Snipers have fired several shots into the Capitol Building itself. Fortunately, no one was hurt. Police and Army units wearing gas masks have fired tear gas at the rioters, but the wind keeps blowing the gas back into the Capitol. The police had to quit using tear gas, or Congress would have to adjourn. There is speculation that if things get worse, Congress may have to flee Washington, D.C. again and set up shop somewhere else.

The next part of the news deals with economic news. For the first time anyone can remember, the Dow Jones is diving below 1,500. Investors, nervous over the continued rioting and unrest, continue to sell; the market continues the slow decline that started in 1999 and has gone on unabated ever since.

The only good news is hearing how the L.A. City Council set up the lottery for the folks burned out in the fires. I hope that will be enough to slow down the unrest and bring even more people back to work on our project.

Anyway, enough news. I get up from my chair in our tent and tell everybody I'll be back in a little while. It's time to see if they'll let me in to see Holly. I've been there four times this afternoon and evening – but to no avail.

When I get to the quarantine tent, Naomi's outside. First time I've caught up with her all day. She's talking to a black couple who looks to be in their mid-forties.

"Hi, Jason. These are Holly's parents, Mr. and Mrs. Jackson." I shake hands with Mr. Jackson, a solid looking man dressed in a tweed sport jacket and blue jeans. He has a gentle smile and a firm handshake. Mrs. Jackson, a tall robust woman, puts her long arms around me and gives me a long hug.

"I called them this afternoon," Naomi says. "They were here within the hour."

"Mr. and Mrs. Jackson, I'm most glad to meet you. My name is Jason Mann. I'm a friend, a really good friend, of Holly's. In fact, I think I'm Holly's boyfriend, but I'm not sure. Anyway, she's not sure, but I think I am." Both Jacksons laugh, and I turn away feeling totally embarrassed. Fortunately, like Holly, her parents seem to have a good sense of humor. After shaking my hand, they just stand there for several seconds smiling at me. At least my awkwardness has managed to take some of the seriousness out of the situation.

"Each of you will have to wear a mask." Naomi breaks the moment of silence and my embarrassment. "This is only precautionary. We still haven't heard anything from the hospital on the tests they took the other day. Come on. Let's all go in. You, too, Jason." Naomi grabs my arm and pulls me along.

I look around and count ten patients, about half from our community and half from the Sacramento group. Ron, our doctor, is examining Marv near the end of the row of bunks. They both look up and wave, and then the doctor goes on with his exam.

Holly's bunk is in the middle. She's reading and doesn't notice us until we're almost up to her. "Dad! Mom! How did you know I was sick? I didn't see you guys come in."

"Oh, an angel of mercy phoned up today," Mr. Jackson says, trying to be lighthearted. "You should've called us days ago, Holly. We haven't heard from you in weeks. We've been worried, and I guess with good reason." Then Holly's mom rushes up to Holly and gives her a long hug.

I realize Holly hasn't noticed me yet, so instead of interrupting her and her parents, I turn away and walk over to Naomi who's standing by herself near the doorway to the tent watching it all. "Where have you been, Naomi?" I say rather scoldingly. "I looked for you all day."

"I've been here, helping Dr. Ron. I guess in all the uproar I forgot to tell you. I'm his new Nurse Assistant. I never told you. I worked two years at our community hospital for my volunteer time. I'm a real nurse. Aren't you impressed?"

"I guess so, but aren't you worried about getting sick? I mean, I am really glad you're here with Holly, but TB is supposed to be really infectious. Do you know what you're doing?"

"Calm down, Jason. I know what I'm doing. I am fine. We have surgical masks, and I've been wearing one all the time. Besides, someone had to help, and I couldn't stand the thought of Holly and the others feeling stranded here by themselves. It's really okay, Jason. I'm fine."

I put my arms around Naomi and give her a hug. I look over her shoulder at Holly who is busy telling her parents of her last two weeks of adventure. Holly glances around her mom's shoulder, gives me a smile and a wink.

"Naomi, I think I'll get a bite to eat and get some sleep. I am really exhausted. I might be back a little later this evening. Tell Holly, okay?"

"All right. But Jason, are you okay?"

"I'm fine." With that, I walk out of the tent, deciding it's a little late for dinner, and I'm tired and feeling disoriented. So maybe I'll just go to bed.

It is well past midnight. I am not able to sleep. It's strange to be lying here in my bunk knowing that Holly and Naomi are not in theirs. The strangest dream woke me. It was about Holly being carried off by giant rats. I shake my head, get off my bunk, pull on my pants, and walk outside to try to clear my head. I stare off into the sky, looking for a star to give me guidance.

One lonesome star manages to struggle through the dense haze and twinkles off the west. This is the first night since I've left Higher Ground that I really feel lonely and homesick. I hadn't realized how much I have come to depend on Holly and Naomi's friendship. I feel close to everyone in our group, especially Philip, but it's different with the three of us. The Three Musketeers – that's what Bob had called us... seems like a lifetime ago. Now one of us is sick, perhaps very sick. I don't think Naomi would have Holly's parents come if she wasn't really worried.

I miss Holly like crazy. *Do I really love her? Romantically?* I think I do. I had never thought much about Holly being black until she mentioned it the other day. There are several hundred black people at Higher Ground and I have never really even thought of them being different until I left the community and came to Watts.

Bob and Becky Houser – she's black and he's white, but I'd never given that aspect much thought, never heard anyone else mention it either. Bob and Becky live just down a couple of doors from my dad, and always seem to get along fine. Somehow, when you're taught to love unconditionally, you just never think of the color of another's skin. It seems that here in urban America the skin color is indeed a very big deal. A guy could get killed for just being the wrong color. It's certainly crazy. And it's going to have to change or this whole place is going to explode right off the planet. We need a new vision.

I guess that's what we're doing here in Watts. We've got our vision and we've certainly had our setbacks, but we're not giving up. We're just going ahead slowly, biding our time, waiting 'til we get back on track. Then watch out! I can feel that it's all going to come together if we just don't give up and keep focused.

I look at my watch. Time for sleep... past midnight, but I am not even tired. Didn't get anything figured out about Holly, but I feel better. *I can't worry about her. I have to let it go. I just have to trust, keep the faith. Tomorrow will be a new day.* I give one last glance at my star and say a quick prayer, knowing that all I have to do is trust.

Then it hits me like a bolt of lightning. *I've got to find out what those tests say. I can't wait. Just this once – to heck with the trusting process.*

> The doctor of the future will give
> no medicine but will interest
> his patients in the care of
> the human frame, in diet, and in the
> cause and prevention of disease.
>
> Thomas Edison

# Chapter 13

The night is warm, must still be in the eighties. There is almost a full moon and, with the bright neon lights of the city, it seems almost like daylight. If I could only read the street signs, I'd be okay. Many of them are just plain gone, while some of them have so many bullet holes in them that I can't make out the letters. To top it off, the city must have forgotten to pay its power bill as none of the street lights work. Even with the light of the moon, I'm lost.

The directions said north on Eight Street until I get to Downey Street, but which one is Downey Street? It's a different world out here. There are lots of folks moving about – like a party on every corner. I haven't met a white face since I left an hour ago. There must be a liquor store on every corner, with a pawnshop and a bar next door. Holly told me that this was the toughest part of L.A., and I can see why. It even smells tough – like stale cigar smoke.

Luella told me that most self-respecting black people would not even come down here – that this was the part of town that should have burned down. I'm getting some strange looks, but no one has said a word to me. I've asked several people for directions, but they just kept walking without even turning around. I've heard several shots that didn't sound too far away, but I just keep on moving north. I am at another corner with no street sign. I assume I must be getting near Downey Street, and the hospital is supposed to be just a few blocks down.

"Hey you, whitey! You remember us?"

Sitting on a curb under the dim light of Joe's Liquor Store I see a familiar looking group of teenagers staring at me as I walk. Suddenly, two of them get up and start walking toward me at almost a lope. I look around for help, but it's obvious I am on my own. I head off in a full gallop up what I hope is Downey Street.

*Whomp!* I remember hitting the pavement. I can't seem to get my bearings. My legs ache, and I can't seem to move them.

"Hey, I am really sorry," some woman is saying to me, almost like she is talking to me from another planet. "But you ran right in front of me." I keep hearing this distant voice. "You ran right in front of me! I didn't even get a chance to hit my brakes."

I struggle to open my eyes and get focused. I can see a crowd around me. A large dark woman with a worried-looking face hovers above me. She keeps talking a mile a minute, and she pleads with the bystanders, "You saw it, didn't you? I couldn't stop! He ran right in front of me. There was nothing I could do!"

I can feel some tingling in my legs, and I don't know why, but I must get up. Slowly, I roll over onto my knees and try putting one foot on the ground under me. Like a drunken sailor, I topple over onto my side. *God! This pavement is hard!*

"We'll take care of him," I hear a male voice say. "We'll take him with us and get him all doctored up so we can tie him to the bumper of a car and drag him through the streets of Watts."

"Hey, man. Remember, we don't have no car left," whines another youth standing over me, poking my stomach with the toe of his boot. "Man, they stoned our car and set it afire, all because of this honkey boy here. Let's just do him right here."

"You boys get away from the white boy. I hit him. He's my responsibility," says the woman driver, her face now very stern as she steps between my assailants and me. If he dies, his relatives will sue me for everything I've got and take away my cab. Now, you boy, help me put him in my cab. I'm taking him to the hospital. There ain't so sense calling an ambulance 'cause they won't leave that hospital with all this shooting going on."

"We ain't putting that son-of-a-bitch in the back of your cab, lady. Ain't no way. We'll just stomp him to death right here, and then you won't have to worry about him no more," answers one of the posse.

"You boys must have misunderstood me! And you're starting to piss me off. I wasn't asking; I was telling. Now get this boy in the back of my cab before I really lose my temper, and then I'll be taking *all* of you to the hospital... as patients. Now get going! Pick that boy up – and not by his nostrils. Be gentle," she bellows as she stands with her hands on hips, legs spread apart.

Much to my surprise, I'm hoisted by my arms and dumped not too gently into the back seat of the cab by my two would-be assassins. "We'll get you, White Boy. I promise! We'll get you," the leader snarls as he shoves my legs into the back seat. "We'll be waiting at the hospital door when you get out, and we'll make sure they put you right back in." Those were the last words I remember.

Now I'm being picked up and put onto a stretcher and rolled into a room with lots of lights and people peering into my face. I try to talk, but keep drifting off. I hear a doctor say, "He's going to be all right. A concussion – but not a serious one. Nothing seems to be broken. Put him in with the others. He'll be able to leave after we watch him for a

179

couple of hours. See if you can find out if he has any relatives or friends nearby."

I'm wheeled into a room with lots of other people, all on portable beds just like mine. I slowly sit up and look around. My head still hurts, but it's clearing. The hospital appears to be in chaos, people going in every direction. Patients on carts like mine are stuck or fit into small pieces of space. Several patients covered with blood get wheeled past me, into the room I just came from. I hear an orderly say, "It's a war zone out there – a bloody war zone."

*A war zone. Yes.* Even the hospital seems like a war zone – emergency after emergency coming in right before my eyes. From the talk I hear, most of the injuries seem to be gunshot or knife wounds. I guess I'm lucky. I've spent my whole life being sheltered from violence, but now it's getting nearer by the moment. It's a sick yet exciting feeling, like what you'd expect from taking drugs. That's what my dad said violence was, like a drug – a drug used to insulate one from having to feel, to care, to love; a drug to break the boredom, to release the frustration of lives that have lost meaning; a drug that doesn't ask why things aren't the way they're supposed to be.

*Enough philosophizing. I've got to get up and find out about Holly.* I had almost forgotten that's why I am here. I definitely feel better – just a big headache and a little dizziness. *One foot down after another – there, I'm standing now. If I just can find someone in this bedlam who can tell me how to find out information about tests.*

I talk to at least a half dozen nurses, several doctors, and one administrator. They all tell me they're too busy, they can't help me, to come back in the morning.

I'll have to spend the night here. I can't make it back to our camp. I notice my cot is still empty. Things are slowing down a bit, probably because it's now past midnight. I push my cot over into a corner behind some plants and climb on.

This guy next to me looks really out of it; I wonder what happened to his head. The hospital is noisy, a constant background music of sirens and helicopters. I'm really tired and sore; sleep is coming eagerly.

"Hey! Where are you taking me! You can't do this! Sir! Miss! You can't do this! You can stop right now! I am okay!"

*How come they can't hear me? How come I am strapped to the gurney? What is happening? Am I dreaming? Is this a nightmare? These lights — they're so bright! There must be a million of them. My God! This is an operating room! Who are these people in blue gowns?*

"I am okay! You can't do this to me! Really! I am okay. Listen to me, please! NO! NO! I don't want that needle in my arm! Get away! I am going to scream! Help! Help!"

"Jesus, what's going on here? Who is this guy?"

"I'm Jason – Jason Mann, and who are you? What are you trying to do to me?" I scream as I kick my feet, and a harried male nurse tries to undo the straps holding me down. The anesthesiologist just stands there with his mouth hanging open and the needle dangling from his left hand. My teeth are chattering so badly that I hardly have control of my mouth, but at least my hands are free to move. "Oh my, oh my," is all I can say. The nurses and doctor just stare at me like I'm some type of alien being. They seem frozen in place, like porcelain dolls unable to speak, move or even close their mouths that still gape open.

"I am standing up. I can stand up. You didn't operate on me, right?"

"No, we didn't operate. You're okay."

A female nurse pulls down her mask, slips off her cap and almost shrieks, "How did you get in here? What did you do with Mr. Janson?"

"Me? I didn't do anything with anybody! You guys kidnapped me! I was sleeping out there in the lobby minding my own business when all of a sudden I wake up and you guys are ready to dissect me! Geez, I didn't do anything with anybody. I gotta get out of here! Please!"

I make for the door with the red exit sign above it, almost reach it. Then I realize all I am wearing is a hospital gown open in the back. I stop short and turn around. Everyone is simply standing still staring at me, but at least the anesthesiologist has put down his needle. Grabbing my pants that are hanging from a coat rack near the exit, I yell, "Good night" as I sprint out the door before anyone has second thoughts about trying that again.

*Wow!* I think to myself as I put on my pants in the men's lavatory. *Was I lucky!* Or maybe unlucky in the first place, but I am glad to be out of there with my head attached. I still can't figure out what was going on. Maybe they mistook me for that guy next to me with the bruises on his head.

*Man, am I stiff! I've never felt so stiff in my life.* My body aches from toes to my head. Don't know if it's from the accident or sleeping on the hospital cot before they dragged me in there. I feel rather rumpled and battered, but no one seems to notice. Things seem a lot slower around here this morning. All the cots are empty. I wonder what happened to that Janson fellow.

The first thing to do is find someone in charge who can help me. I remember the door from last night that said Hospital Information. So, still shaking, I walk back down the hallway until I find the room. *Thank goodness.* Someone's inside the glass door.

I introduce myself to an office administrator who seems to be the lady I've been looking for. She is a middle-aged, happy-faced, heavy-set woman whose nametag says *Mrs. Carson.* When I tell her my plight, she's eager to help, although I'm afraid I might get in trouble if I tell her about the surgery room.

She introduces me to Dr. Benson, a young, serious, looking black doctor who, with a concerned look, introduces himself as the emergency doctor on duty.

"Come into my office, Jason. Sit down," says Dr. Benson. "You look a little peaked. Are you okay?"

"I'm fine," I answer tight-lipped, my heart pounding.

"Actually, it seems that the tests have been back at the hospital for several days. I don't know why they didn't send them to your community doctor. It's just that we've been in such chaos here. It takes a week to get the mail open. I had an orderly bring over the tests. Let's see what we have here. These are your friend's – Holly's – x-rays and test results. They are negative for both tuberculosis and lung cancer. And I don't see any signs of any Bacterial Bacteriophage. It's the same for everyone else we tested in your group. Also their blood and urine tests – all negative.

"It looks to me like she has picked up a mild lung infection. It's getting to be very common among folks who first move into the urban area or who have been gone for a length of time and then come back. It's similar to the old black lung disease which coal miners used to get in the 1800's, but not as serious. Generally, blacks seem to be more susceptible – though we don't know why yet.

"This time it's the smog and smoke that's the culprit. It coats the lungs and causes irritations and reactions much like an allergy. The actual problem is not that serious in the short term. It's that people's immune systems get worn down and they become susceptible to the barrage of viruses going around. To make it worse, these viruses have become immune to our drugs, so it's almost useless to give drugs anymore. That's what half the people in this hospital are here for right now. It's up to the patients to take better care of themselves and not depend on drugs or doctors so much. It's more like another warning sent by our ecosystem that we're living in a very unhealthy environment."

"Dr. Benson, what can I do to help them?" I ask impatiently.

"I advise your friend Holly and the others to just take it easy. Treat their symptoms the same as asthma or an extreme allergy outbreak. Once their system gets used to the high pollutants, most of their symptoms should go away. What they all have to remember – as do the rest of us – is that we're all just like rats in a laboratory. We don't know for sure what tolerance each of us has for the heavy doses of toxic pollutants we receive each day as city dwellers. But what we do know is that your chances are 80 percent better of getting cancer living in L.A. than if you were 100 miles east of here in the Mojave Desert."

*Great. What are we doing here?*

"So, good luck to your friends, and to you, too," he says as he stands up. "Keep up the good work building those tire houses. They're the best things that have ever happened to the city – particularly Watts. Good-bye and good luck." Dr. Benson shakes my hand, looks at me awkwardly, and then we both smile and give each other a hug.

My aches are gone. My head feels like new. *This was all just a bad dream. Holly's okay! They're all okay!* I am out of here. Got to get back and give everyone the news. I thank Dr. Benson again as I head for the nearest exit sign.

I just get outside and am trying to get my bearings when I hear, "Hey, White Boy. Look behind you."

*Oh, shit!* I had forgotten about the threat the posse members had left me with after they so gently dumped me in the back of the cab. I turn around with a sick feeling in my stomach and weary legs prepared for flight.

"Hey, White Boy. Don't look so alarmed. We're just here to check up on you and make sure you made it here okay. We're going to make sure you make it home okay too. We're your guardian angels," the pony-tailed black man says with a grin. I just stand there with my mouth wide open.

"Hop in the back seat. We don't have much gas. Who can afford it at $6 a gallon? Don't worry about your friends from Compton," laughs Clyde. "We saw them hanging around here this morning waiting to walk you home. We thanked them, but we told them you didn't need their services – The Avengers were here to give you a ride home. They told us to tell you best of luck and that you wouldn't be seeing them any more as they had business elsewhere."

All three of The Avengers laugh as they look at each other, and then we drive off from the hospital in what Clyde tells me is a black '99 Ford Tempo lowered just about to the ground. The inside of this vehicle is like nothing I have ever experienced before. The seats and dash are smooth black leather. Black curtains hang from atop the side windows. The carpet is black, as plush as the headliner above. Everything's black, including the black-handled revolver hanging in a holster on the driver's door!

"What brought you guys to the hospital?" I finally stammer as we're on our way back to Watts.

"Well, man, it was like this," says Clyde as he turns around from the passenger's seat and faces me. "Your little white girlfriend, Naomi, came out to the street this morning just before we left our guard duty. Said you had left last night to find out about Holly and hadn't returned. She told us about your run-in with those brothers from Compton. Sounded like those boys might still be looking for you. So we thought we'd cruise over to the hospital and see if you were still alive, maybe get in a little action out of our Compton brothers. They didn't want to play, so we just waited around for you, and here we are."

"Action? What were you going to play?" I ask Clyde, not exactly sure what he is talking about. "I mean, with your Compton brothers. What game do you play?"

Clyde laughs sarcastically. "We play hardball, White Boy. Plain, simple hardball. Those dudes don't get out of our way, we hit them with a bat. They give us a hard time or fight back, we shoot at them, they shoot at us. We call it hardball."

"You shoot with real guns?"

"Yeah, White Boy. We shoot with real guns. This is a mean town. You either kill or be killed. Just like in the movies. Only our blood is real when we die. We're dead. I lost my older brother about a year ago." Clyde's voice gets very soft. "Some Mexican from the Midnighters shot him dead. No reason. Just wanted to shoot a black gang member. So he shot and killed my brother right in front of my folk's home. That's the way it is, White Boy. It's insane. It really is insane. Ya know, man, everyone lives in fear down here. It's survival of the fittest, and right now The Avengers are the fittest. So, you've got your protection."

"I really appreciate that," I say, not quite sure what I *should* say. "And I don't mean to sound ungrateful, but I need to know why you helped me. Why do you say I have your protection?"

"White Boy, the word is out on you and your friends." Clyde looks me straight in the eyes. "You're here to help. You haven't judged us or told us how we have to live. You've just taught us how to build better houses and better neighborhoods. You guys are idealistic nuts, but most of us do appreciate what you're doing. I've got a three-year-old son, and I don't want him growing up like me and my friends. Just cuz we're in a gang doesn't mean we're stupid. We all know if this shit keeps going on, there ain't gonna be nothing left but a bunch of dead niggers, Mexicans, and white boys. So you guys keep building your spaceships, or whatever you call those things, and we'll keep your white asses safe."

Before I can collect my thoughts and reply, Clyde says, "Here you are, White Boy. You're home. And by the way, say 'hello' to sister Holly for me. We used to get together a couple of years ago – back in high school."

With that, the passenger door is opened and before I can say thanks, they're gone – heading down the road in a cloud of gray exhaust. *I'm okay. I made it back alive. I can't believe it!*

I'm left standing on our perimeter road outside our earthships. What an amazing twenty-four hours. I've been run over by a cab, had a posse want to murder me, spent the night on a cot in a hospital jammed with people, almost got my brain operated on, and now I get rescued by another gang whose leader turns out to be Holly's ex-boyfriend. Yep, this has been the worst twenty-four hours of my life. *I just hope I don't have another day quite so exciting again for a long time. From now on, I think I'll go back to letting the universe run things, and I'll just rely on trust.*

I watch the black Ford drive completely out of sight and immediately turn and head in a trot towards the quarantine tent. I pass our construction site and can see we're getting back into full swing. Thousands of workers up and down the block are working on dozens of earthships. I don't want to be recognized as I don't want to take the time to stop and talk. So I put my head down and jog past our construction site until I reach our tent.

Help thy brother's boat across
and lo, thine own
has reached the shore.

Hindu Proverb

# Chapter 14

Have I lost my bearings or maybe my marbles? There is no quarantine tent. Maybe the sign's just gone. I look up and down the row of tents and know the one I am standing in front of has to be the right one. I open the tent flap and peek in, but the tent is empty, except for the rows of beds and lockers. I turn and look up and down the pathway between the rows of tents. This certainly is the right tent, but no Holly, Naomi, or anyone else. How could everything change in just twenty-four hours?

I almost gallop over to the tent where we've been living and go inside. It too is devoid of people, but all our belongings are here just like when I left. *Where are Holly and Naomi?* I risked my life to find out about Holly's tests, and now she and everyone else is gone. *God, could they have been kidnapped?*

My stomach churns as I walk back out into the warm sunshine. The temperature on the thermometer attached to the tent pole says it's already in the 90's. My watch shows that it is noon. I look up and down the row of tents but see not a soul. *Where could everyone have gone? What do I do?*

I decide to go back to our earthship construction site and find out if anyone there knows what has happened to Holly and the others. I find myself trotting again, and it takes only several minutes to get there. As I trot up, I feel the sweat already starting to drip into my eyes.

"Hey, Jason!" *Thank goodness! It's Naomi.* "Over here."

I stop, turn and see her and Holly casually standing next to a half-finished earthship. Out of breath, I hear myself almost screech, "What are you guys doing over here? Holly, you're supposed to be in bed! What happened to the quarantine tent? What's going on here?"

"Jason, it's okay," says Naomi, "Calm down. This morning we got a letter from the testing laboratory. Actually, it had been sitting in our box for a couple of days. No one had thought of going over and checking it. We all thought someone else had done it. Everyone's okay, Jason. Isn't that great?"

"You mean," I ask in utter disbelief, "I risked my life, and we already had a letter from the laboratory? And what're you and Nate and the rest of the sick people doing out here?" Then I turn towards Holly. "You guys are supposed to still be resting – not out here pounding tires."

"Look, Jason," Holly says, "I am not going to sit in that old tent now that I know I am not dying. That's the way Nate and the rest feel too. We're going to be out in the sunshine working and doing the best we can. So, White Boy, calm yourself down and tell us what happened. We've been worried sick about you. Where have you been?"

"Where have I been?" *What an anti-climax.* I lean against the tire house. I had pictured myself rushing into Holly's tent, telling everyone that everything was okay. Exuberance would have broken out, Holly throwing herself into my arms in appreciation. At least, that's the way I had it figured.

So I spend the next half-hour unenthusiastically telling anyone who will listen about my adventure. Everyone listens patiently, congratulates me for making it back alive, and then goes quietly back to work – everyone, that is, but Holly. She just stands there in her tank top and shorts, her arms folded, her face rather serious, staring at me as if she's seeing me for the first time.

Finally, after everyone's gone, she says, "Jason, you really did risk your life for me. I mean, because you had to know how sick I really was. I guess no one's ever done anything like that for me before." She puts her hands on my waist and gently pulls me to her. Her warm lips quickly press against mine for what seems like only an instant. It's all I can do to open my eyes to find out why that wonderful feeling has stopped. I feel dizzy and can barely stand. But Holly has turned away and is already headed back to work.

As she walks away, she turns her head and says with a large smile, "Bye, White Boy. See you after dinner."

I stand glazed for a moment. When my mind turns back on, I realize we are entering a new stage of our relationship. As I watch her walk away, gently swaying back and forth in her blue jeans shorts, I still smell her perfume in the air. *Yes! I am in trouble.*

As I awaken from my trance, I see... thousands of people working on earthships, rec centers, and the parks around them. As I look around, I see more neighborhood people coming back to the work sites, just grabbing tools and going to work. I can feel the momentum in the air. This time it seems more permanent though, like we really know why we're doing it. It's what Bob said about us doing something really good – it seems to be happening.

"Hey, Jason. Glad to see you back," says Brad, grinning as he walks up and gives me a hug.

"Glad to be back, Brad. I think working on earthships is a lot easier and safer than running around the streets of this town. Looks like things are really starting to move again. With all the people hustling around, this place is starting to look like a real community."

"Yes. It really does. The city is supposed to hold its first lottery this Friday for 100 of the earthships. People could actually be living here in another two weeks, and that is exciting," he says as he puts his hand on my shoulder.

"I am glad to hear that Holly, Nate, and the others don't have anything real serious," he continues. "Looks, though, like Holly may have a pretty serious case of infatuation. It must be contagious too, because you look like you're coming down with the same symptoms."

We both laugh. "I guess I do, Brad. Not quite sure what to do with it though. This is all new to me."

"It's always new to any of us, *anytime* it happens. Just don't let that old fear out here in this world come into it. I find it hard to go about my business here in L.A. without fear somehow entering into it someplace. I don't like it."

"Me too," I say. "Though I feel like there's a change coming. I really do. I can feel it, even smell it in the air. It's like a new hope is arising from the ashes of Watts, and it's going to spread over the whole nation."

"Yes, I think you're right, Mr. Philosopher. I feel the same way. But maybe I'm in love, too!"

We both laugh, put our arms over each other's shoulder, and head for lunch and an hour's siesta.

# Chapter 15

"You're an old stick-in-the-mud, Jason. Of course, we need a party," Holly says as a bunch of us sit in front of our tent enjoying a Saturday morning off. Four weeks have gone by since we started back on the earthships and things are going well.

"We've got lots of reasons to celebrate. We've got over 3,000 earthships completed. Our community is three-quarters finished. People have moved in, and this place is becoming a real community. I just read in the paper that people all over the country have really noticed what we're doing, and they're at least talking about building new communities in many of the major cities."

"Yes," adds Ami, "we've been on every major news show in the country and maybe the world."

"And," says Naomi, "the rioting has almost stopped. Not much smoke, not nearly as many shootings."

"The President has gotten most of her agenda through Congress, and her plans seem to be working – or at least the unemployment rate dropped two percent in June, even after raising the minimum wage," Philip tells me. "So much for those pessimists saying it would rise 10 percent. Plus, the economy is really pushing up with all the money circulating. It's starting to make a difference."

"Even the murder rate has dropped," Naomi says.

"Yeah," Brad says, "there were only half as many murders in the country this month as last,"

Holly stands up. "Oh, you two guys are too gloomy. Things really are getting better. Both you guys are stealing our energy instead of giving us more. You guys need to get with the program. So what does everybody think? Do we have a party or not?"

"You've got me convinced. I'm in," Brad says.

I'm easily swayed. "Me, too... I guess. Let's get busy and start organizing, if we're going to do this. How about you, Philip?" *As if I really needed to ask.*

"Count me in. I am all for a party. Let's do it."

"I think this party needs to be a gigantic street party, with everybody from Watts and all the people who have worked on the community participating." says Holly, walking in a circle, her hands moving as fast as her mouth.

I tell Holly that's impossible. "You'd have gangs, soldiers, police, blacks, whites, and Latinos, all partying together. It would be bedlam, at best."

"Come on, Jason. I know what you mean, something does feel out of sync, but we'll figure it out as we go along," Naomi says with a question on her face.

"It would bring everyone together. It would show the whole world we can do this, that everyone can cooperate and live in love instead of fear. I think we ought to go for it," says Ami.

Brad and I look at each other and shrug. *Am I just coming from fear?* I can't tell, but something isn't registering right.

We look over at Philip, who gives us the thumbs up. "Let's do it," he says. "If we really believe what we say, and we walk what we talk, it's worth the chance."

It still doesn't feel right, but I hear myself reluctantly saying, "Okay, I'm in. So where do we go from here?"

"Well, first I think we need to approach our whole community and make sure we're in consensus," Naomi says.

"Then we need to form some committees to work on food and entertainment. I have a pad of paper here, and we can start making a list of everything we're going to need. We'll ask for a group meeting tonight after dinner. We feel if our community will sponsor the idea, the rest of the communities will support it."

After two weeks of planning, the day's arrived: July 4th, 2012. It's going to be a warm one with the predicted  temperature in the 90's.  The smog doesn't look like it's going to be too bad. The slight breeze coming in off the ocean brings a smell of salt air and helps to keep the haze out.

Holly and Naomi have been in an uproar for two weeks, ever since all of the groups involved had finally agreed a celebration party was in order. The two of them have taken on the responsibility of making this party happen almost solely by themselves. The rest of us have been busily working ten-hour days on the earthships while they organize the party.

I haven't seen Holly much in the last two weeks. In fact, I haven't seen much of her since my adventure to the hospital well over a month ago. We've both been really busy working six days a week, but I don't think that's the main reason. I think there has been reluctance on both our parts to take the next step from friends to lovers. For myself, it's a gigantic step, and one that I have been unable to get myself to make. Maybe after the party things will slow down and give us some time alone.

Naomi, Holly, Brad, and I find ourselves making last-minute checks an hour before people are to start arriving.

"We have five bands. Each one will be playing on a different street," Naomi says as we stand in a parkway running between two rows of earthships. "Each street will have at least one earthship open as a model for people to see the final product. We're going to barbecue 10,000 hot dogs and hamburgers and will serve over 2,000 pounds of donated potato salad. People will be bringing their own drinks, and we asked everyone to bring a dessert. Phil's group is putting up signs saying *No Drugs or Alcohol Allowed.*

"That should help with the security problems," Holly says. "I got Clyde and representatives from almost every gang in Watts and Compton to serve as security leaders, making sure things don't get out of hand. We'll have over 400 gang members and even some posse members wearing white armbands circulating throughout the crowds, just talking and keeping things cool. They'll be in pairs, but no two members from the same gang will be working together. Clyde thought that would ease the tension of the us-against-them mentality."

"We've got fireworks to start at 10:00," states Brad. "That should last about an hour, and then hopefully everyone will go home. Hopefully."

The four of us stand up from the floor of the near-empty rec room, hold hands for a minute, do a silent meditation, and head out the door. The party is about to begin, and people are starting to drift in from the surrounding neighborhoods. The bands, mostly rock and folk bands from around the L.A. area, are starting to warm up. Watts is slipping into a cautiously festive mood.

"Hey, Holly!" We both turn around and see Clyde walking up.

"Jason, you remember Clyde. You met him about a month ago," she says laughing as he walks up to us from what seems like out of nowhere.

"Sure do. I might not be here if it weren't for him."

We look at each other for a moment, and then give each other an awkward hug instead of a handshake.

"Man, am I glad I ended up picking you up that morning, Jason. Otherwise, I wouldn't have had the chance to see Holly again." Clyde looks over at Holly with a smile and a certain look in his eyes. *This guy's not over her. I could be in for some competition.*

Holly appears not to notice Clyde's admiring look and keeps right on chattering away about the party. Eventually, she puts one of her arms through mine, the other through Clyde's, and we stroll down the new parkway of what was once called Watts and is now Los Miracles.

"Everyone looks so happy, the bands playing, people starting to dance – it seems like a carnival," Holly says. "I can smell cotton candy from one of the booths. So which one of you guys is a dancer?"

I look at Clyde and he smiles, "Lady," he says to Holly, "I was born to dance. Don't you remember high school? I was a dancing fool."

"I do remember you being a fool." She wrinkles her nose. "And I guess I do remember you being a good dancer. How about you, White Boy? Do you guys ever dance in your community?"

"Sure, Holly, we dance all the time," I say rather hesitantly, "but I have never considered myself a really good dancer."

As I look around at the neighborhood, people are dancing in what used to be a street and now is a basketball court. I'm out of my league. These people have rhythm and coordination – two characteristics I seem to have been born without.

"I dance," I continue. "I am not great, but I like to dance. But I think I'd better go find Naomi and help her cook hot dogs. See you guys later." After a wave from Clyde, and a frown from Holly, I make my way through the gathering crowd.

*It's strange,* I think, *to see Holly with Clyde.* A little jealousy's another new feeling for me. I can't tell by Holly's attitude how she feels about Clyde, but they are sure a lot better friends than when they met on the street corner two months ago. One thing for sure: I am not going to get in a dance competition with Clyde. I'll go cook hot dogs. I can tell from the smell that there is a booth not too far away.

"Hey Jason, how'd we get the job of cooking hot dogs? I'm a vegetarian. I don't even eat these things," says Naomi, standing behind a large metal drum cut in half and filled with hot charcoals.

Cliff, who's helping Naomi cook, laughs. "You white folks are not hot dog connoisseurs, I can tell that. If I had known, I'd have brought some tofu burgers. Then you folks would feel right at home," he says with a grin.

"You bet," Naomi says. "Give me a tofu burger, black beans, some apple cider, and I'd be as happy as a bear in a blackberry patch."

Cliff laughs and says, "Well, young lady, we got lots of pork and beans, but we forgot about the pork being meat. Next time we do this, we'll have garden burgers and tofu, I promise."

The intensity of the music has been rising right along with the temperature. The crowds are thickening, and the dancing has spread up the parkways between the earthships. There's a gentle festive mood. A change seems to be taking place right before our eyes – not a measurable change, but one that is being blown in with the gentle breeze off the Pacific. Call it a wind of lightheartedness, of hope for changes. Marv used to tell us in school that changes can start ever so slowly yet be so massive that a single mind cannot possible comprehend their implication.

Standing behind my grill, I sense a peacefulness I have not felt since I left Higher Ground many months ago. As I sway to the music, I see Naomi holding hands with Brad. Her broad smile says that she too is carefree and joyous.

*What's that?* I jump! Two hands are placed on my waist from behind. "Hi, Jason. I didn't know you were a chef," laughs Holly. "Especially a chef who can dance while he cooks. I like that they teach men to cook where you come from. That's a good sign."

Naomi looks over from her cooking duties and laughs with Holly at what I feel is my expense. I turn red, get distracted, and drop several hot dogs through the grill onto the hot coals below.

"Go on, Jason. Why don't you go with Holly for a while?" Naomi says. "Otherwise, I think we're going to run out of hot dogs. Philip, Ami and Brad are here now to help. We can handle these dogs."

"I'll cook them, but I'm not sure I'll eat them," laughs Philip, as I hand him my turning tongs.

"Come on, Jason." Holly grabs my hand and drags me into the moving mass of humanity. "This is our day off and a chance to do something together. It seems like we're never alone, almost like you have been avoiding me this last month."

"I thought you were avoiding me," I blurt out. "I wasn't... I'm not sure what is happening between you and Clyde. It seems like you two have gotten really close lately, and I don't want to be in the way."

"Hmm. After all you told me about your community, I thought you guys were enlightened on the subject of relationships. Clyde and I are just friends, nothing more. He told me he was interested in more, and I told him I was after your bod so I wasn't available. He made a joke, (at least I think it was a joke), saying he wasn't so glad he picked you up at the hospital after all, but that he'd get over it.

"I think he really just thinks of me like a sister now. He just hasn't figured that totally out yet. I hooked Clyde up with Jess, and they're around here somewhere patrolling the parkways."

"Oh."

"'Oh'? That's all you have to say? Come on, Jason. Get a life." Holly pulls me by the hand into an empty earthship.

There are several other people wandering around inside checking it out, but they pay us little attention. The air feels cool inside, until Holly again slides her arms around my waist. This time her lips find mine. This kiss is longer and more passionate than the one a month ago. Her body presses close to mine, and I am lost in a sea of warmth and passion.

"Holly," I whisper as our lips part.

"Yes, Jason?"

"Well, I think you're special. You do know that, don't you?"

"Yes, Jason. I figured that out by the way you kissed me. But go on."

"Well, I... it's sure getting warm in here for being so cool."

"Say that again?"

"I don't think so. It isn't important. There's sure getting to be a lot of people in here," I say. We both look around, and the earthship is filling up. The temperature must be in the 90's outside by now, and people are looking for shade inside the cool earthships.

"We've definitely picked up an audience," says Holly. "I guess we might as well walk for a while. It'll be dark in a couple of hours, and then we'll have the fireworks."

We hold hands as we walk through the crowded parkway. Then Holly pulls her hand gently away from mine and turns toward me. "I gotta tell you something," she says.

*This must be serious stuff.* Her face looks vulnerable and wide-eyed, like she expects to be eaten by a hungry lion, and maybe I am the lion. She keeps twisting her hands nervously in front of her chest.

"Jason, it's about how things used to be between Clyde and me, back in high school. Well, uh... guess I'll just get it out on the table, and you can do with it what you want. When I was a junior, I got pregnant; Clyde was the father. I was going to have an abortion, but we changed our minds at the last moment. I just couldn't do it. We have a little boy, three years old. Clyde's mother, Jane... she has baby Chris. She's been pretty much raising him as hers these last three years." Holly's eyes look like they're going to pop right out of her sockets as she intensely looks at me. "I was only sixteen when I had little Chris, and I wasn't in a space to take care of him and neither was Clyde. It's worked out pretty well. I go over to see him a couple times a week. Clyde's mom is a great mom to him, and – oh, shit! That's it I guess." Tears fall like raindrops off her chin.

I hold her in my arms and stroke her long, black, silky hair. I am not sure what to say except that it's okay. I keep holding Holly until she silently pulls away, and we start walking again.

People are playing volleyball, basketball, and horse-shoes. Some folks are dancing; others are sitting on the grass visiting and picnicking. Everything seems calm and relaxed. Gang members with white armbands patrol the walkways in pairs, chatting and joking with people as they make their way through the crowds.

Holly and I don't talk much. I guess I need to go into my cave before I can figure any of this out. I just know it doesn't change the way I feel about Holly, and I clumsily tell her so. After that, we are content just to walk and hold hands. People we have worked with on the tire houses call to us when we walk by. We wave back, go over and chat for a while, and then continue meandering through the crowded parkways. There are many booths and craft carts that local people have set up.

We walk for over two hours, talking to each other and to friends who are scattered through the parkways of what is soon to be Los Miracles.

The fireworks start at 9:45. Holly and I find a place to sit in the grass at the end of a row of earthships. Holly sits back against my knees as we lie in the grass. Even though we're both feeling a little numb and overwhelmed, it is still a perfect ending to what started out being less than a perfect day.

The fireworks have been going for about 15 minutes when I see smoke. It's hard to tell if the smoke is from the fireworks, because the whole horizon seems to be fireworks and its smoky afterwards. But when I focus on one single consistent column of smoke off to the west, I realize it must be coming from one of the earthships.

"Holly! Look! An earthship is on fire! One of those rockets must have landed on something flammable and caught on fire." I jump to my feet and start running through the crowd.

"Jason, wait up," When I look back I see her close behind me, running just as fast as I am. As we run, people start to notice the smoke, then stand up and point it out to others.

Instinctively, I stop, turn to Holly and grab her hand as she tries to pass me. "Slow down," I tell her. "There's something terribly wrong."

We can see another column rising from another earthship. The flames are obvious on this ship and are jumping five to six feet into the air. *What can be causing such a fire?*

We hear the first shots within seconds of arriving at the burning earthships. I grab Holly and throw both of us to the ground. I keep hoping that the shots, which are so numerous, are just another type of fireworks someone is letting off, but my heart knows better.

The flames are spreading over the roof of the two earthships, casting an eerie spell for hundreds of yards in all directions. These earthships have not yet been completed, and the celebration has not extended down this far. There was little reason for anyone to be down here, but now Holly and I can see distant figures moving about against the light of the flames.

I clearly see two people, one with a rifle. We lay frozen to the earth. The man with the rifle must have been shooting, but he seems to have run out of ammunition and is reloading. As I look about, I can only surmise what has happened.

There are several bodies sprawled on the ground between Holly, the two earthships, and me. The bodies are not moving. There is another person who is wearing a mask over his face, and I can see he is carrying some type of container. He tosses his container onto the top of a third earthship, climbs on the low sloping roof and takes out a match.

"Man, you can't do that," Holly yells as she jerks her hand away and springs up.

"Stop!" I scream and jump up. As if in slow motion, the figure with the rifle turns toward Holly's voice and opens fire on Holly and me.

I stand helpless for a second, then throw myself on the ground. I look around for Holly. She seems to have done the same as she is lying flat on the ground ahead of me.

The figure with the rifle momentarily turns his attention away from us as more people come running down the parkway. The figure opens fire again – this time in great spurts that must be from an automatic weapon. I hear screaming and I crawl the remaining feet to Holly. I already know she's been hit... and she doesn't seem to be moving. Time is still going in slow motion, like in a bad nightmare that won't go away. I cover her body with mine, as more bullets whizz overhead.

I hear more yelling and firing. I see Clyde and several gang members with pistols in their hands firing at the figure with the rifle. Clyde goes down, as does another of his gang, but the firing stops. I turn over on my knees; my shirt is covered in blood. I put my head against Holly's chest but can't feel a pulse. Her head is turned sideways and I put my lips to hers and start blowing into her mouth. Her lips are warm but I feel no breath.

"Let me see. Let me help. You have to move away!" a man yells in my ear. I move to one side. A woman comes running to Holly's side and tells the black man with the white armband that she is a nurse.

"Somebody get a medic!" the woman screams. "This one isn't going to make it."

Sirens are coming in every direction. The nurse has ripped Holly's blouse off and is using it to try and stop the bleeding. The man continues to give her CPR. I lie there in the street and shake, unable to stop. I put my hands to my face, and Holly's warm blood covers my eyes. There is a group of mostly black faces standing over me, and they seem paralyzed by the sight of me lying next to Holly's body.

I think I've been lying here a long time. I hear a familiar voice and although I can't seem to open my eyes, I know it's Philip. He has his arm around me and keeps telling me it's going to be okay, but I know it's not. *Holly is dead. She is not coming back to life.* Her blood is on my hands and face, and I can't stop shaking. I can hear voices around me, but they're from a different world.

"Clyde's dead," someone says. "And so is Jess."

Then I hear the nurse say, "She didn't make it."

My shaking starts to mix with tears and I am not sure I will ever stop.

# Chapter 16

"Ladies and gentlemen, the sun is shining out here in Southern California its 11 a.m. Sunday morning. The wind is blowing slightly from the west and it's a beautiful day. I am Josh Richardson from KWTV in Hollywood California. We're standing in front of the Watts Methodist church – a large brick building that is over a hundred years old and can seat several thousand people.

"The President has been speaking for about twenty minutes at the memorial services for the peace corps volunteers killed here in Watts on Sunday. The overflow crowd has spilled out the large double doors. They have listened to her eulogy in stunned silence.

"It looks like the President is now coming out onto the front steps and people are scrambling to give her room. The word is that she told her secret service agents to leave their weapons in a basket in front of the podium. Now one by one the police officers in front of the church are putting their guns in a basket that one of the President's aids is bringing around. The crowed is still very quiet, but there is a low buzz as we all wonder what is going on.

"President Mandell is walking briskly through the crowd on the sidewalk. It appears from where I'm standing across the street, that Reverend Jackson is still with her and so is Jimmy Carter. I also see Cardinal Spellinger and surprisingly

Reverend Marty Karos, considered by many to be a primary spokesman for many of the more conservative fundamental churches across the nation. There must be another hundred spiritual leaders from numerous persuasions that are following close behind. The crowd is amazingly orderly as everyone seems to be spellbound. The President is not heading for her limo but is walking down Hayward street. The crowd is starting to follow her and now we can hear some people starting to sing what sounds like Amazing Grace."

---

"This is a 2 p.m. update from Josh Richardson in Hollywood California. Truly in all my years as a reporter I've never seen anything like this. The President of the United States has already walked for almost three hours now, completely unprotected through one of the roughest cities in the world. More people are coming from every direction and are following along. There must be close to twenty five thousand people in the march at this point. Now millions more are following the procession on television and radio. I don't have any idea where she is going and I don't think the crowds that are gathering know either. They're singing again and the singing is attracting even more people. They've been singing everything from inspirational rock, to Gospel and now it's a Barbara Streisand hit from the late nineties called *Higher Ground.* If she keeps going like the pied piper she may have the whole city following her by nightfall.

They are stopping now, and right in front of the Northgate chapter of the local National Rifle Association building. The President has gotten down on one knee and the crowd is following her example. It looks like they're praying together. Now several men have come out of the building and are joining them.

---

November 7, four months after the shooting

"And I want personally to thank every Congressman and Senator that helped get the final legislation through Congress and the Senate.

"Today is an historic day in America. Martial law has been lifted in Los Angeles, the City of Angels being the last holdout. Reconciliation is sweeping across the nation like we have not seen in our generation, or maybe in any generation. Ladies and Gentlemen, the United States is at peace with the world and more importantly with itself."

---

We're sitting on a pile of tires filled with sand, listening to the President's State of the Union speech from Washington D.C. Peace, she says, is engulfing the land

I may never understand why all this happened. Brad had told me white supremacists set fires to our earthships and how they opened fire on Jess, Clyde, Holly, and me. But at the time I just heard words.

Four days later the President herself addressed the service. Afterwards she told her bodyguards and press people to stay at the Methodist church where the memorial was held. She started walking and people started following, then more and more people. The word kept spreading and the people kept coming. She walked for six hours unattended through the streets of Watts and Compton with tens of thousands of people of all genders and colors following her.

Of all places, we ended up in front of the local headquarters for the National Rifle Association. It had been confirmed that two of the terrorists at the Fourth of July shooting were members. She got down on her knees and led the crowd in a prayer of peace for the nation and us, its people. It was amazing – even the local posse members and winos off the street got down on their knees. She asked the nation to go into three days of mourning, and at the end of those three days for every American to renounce violence in all parts of their lives.

It was like a real miracle. All of a sudden people started getting it. I still don't understand totally why, but they did. It's like a whole new level of optimism filled the air. People started acting friendly and loving to each other in the streets, on the radio and television everywhere. Her "Guns for Lives" program has already collected over two million weapons from around the nation. It's three months later, and it still hasn't stopped.

Holly, Clyde and Jess have all been cremated. It's still hard to accept that they're all gone. In my belief system I trust that their spirits are always with us and that we are still one. But the loss of their physical presence is still sometimes overwhelming.

I miss Holly dearly, but the pain is starting to ease. I feel older, I hope a little wiser. Los Miracles turned out better than I could have ever hoped. Now it's time to go home to Higher Ground.

"Jason, are you ready?" says Naomi as she takes her arm from my shoulder and we both stand up.

Holly's father hands me a vase with Holly's ashes. Cliff carries Clyde's ashes. We thought we would spread some here where the new earthships are being built. I scatter a few ashes and mix them with sand. Cliff and I go to a dozen stacked tires and scatter a little in each. Philip and Floyd, Clyde's best friend, follow silently with shovels and pour sand on top of the ashes. The rest of the ashes we'll take back to Higher Ground and spread them around there. I remember Holly telling me she had been searching for higher ground all her life.

"Hey White Boy," says Cliff, "I am going to miss your lily white face. You folks did a great job. We'll never forget you," he says as he engulfs me in his gigantic arms and doesn't let go for almost a full minute.

Jane, Clyde's mother, is holding little Chris and gives me a kiss on the cheek. "Jason, I promise that I'll bring Chris to the community in the Spring. You sure you want him to stay the summer, though?"

"I am sure, Jane," I tell her, "he'll love it." I look at little Chris as he runs off to play on a swing set up in one of the new parks. He looks a little bit like both of them, I think to myself. Getting to know him has been a real bright spot the last couple of months.

Janet, Holly's mom gives me a long hug and our tears mingle as we hold each other tight. Luella comes up next and looks me in the eye. "Hey, White Boy," she says softly, "it got tough, but we did it." We then hold each other and then she turns away with tears coming down her cheeks.

The bus is pulling out of the parking lot. I strain to take a final look at Los Miracles before it's out of sight. As far as we can see, earthships stand in almost every direction. The California sun is glistening off their solar panels, like bolts of light shooting up into the sky. Children are playing in the parkway; I see a couple of men playing horseshoes and a group of boys playing soccer. We're up on the freeway now, and I turn my head forward and put back my seat to rest. Philip and I look over at each other and give each other a slow affectionate smile.

---

We come to a full stop as Bob prepares to turn left into our lane. Seeing the small brown and white sign that simply says *Higher Ground Community* reminds me how extraordinarily lucky I am to have a community to go home to where I can grieve openly, be loved and totally accepted.

"Jason, we're home," says Naomi as she puts her hand on my shoulders and leans over the back of my seat. "Look at the gold leaves on the aspen trees, they're beautiful. So much has happened in these last seven months it seems more like years. I can't wait to see everyone."

Naomi rubs my shoulders. "Jason, I know it's been tough without Holly, but we have so much to feel good about, with what we've been part of. There's 10,000 people – people who were homeless seven months ago – who have homes, good homes. There's a community out there now, a real community. People's lives are really getting better. Remember how we felt last night when we went to the dedication of the new rec and community center?"

"It was so great," adds Brad sitting next to Naomi. "Really great. Those folks were really taking pride in what they were doing, a real community spirit. It was such a tribute that they named it after Holly and Clyde: The Jackson Clayborn Community Center. I love it."

"That was wonderful," I admit, "though I cried for a half an hour when they told me."

"Me too," Naomi says, new tears rolling down her cheeks. "But it was still great. Neat, the way some of those tough gang members came up and gave us a hug and thanked us. Luella told me that some of them were actually posse members. That was really great."

"Yes, it was. And the way they did that co-op childcare center – it's really going to take a load off those working moms."

Naomi's face is smiling but is still covered in tears. "You know, Jason. I truly believe Holly is with us right now and that she'll always be with us. It's like she's so close I can touch her, and that her spirit goes right on... unless we choose to let it die. I am not exactly sure how it all works, but I know that much."

I know that much too, I think to myself. I look down in my hands at the small gold vase that holds Holly's ashes and, for the first time, I notice the angel imprinted on the side. I remember back to the dream I'd had in L.A. when Kali gave Holly a vase just like this one – and it's then I understand. We really are all coming home together.

I have walked too long in darkness. I have walked too long alone, blindly clutching fists of diamonds that I found were only stones. I would trade the wealth of ages for a warmer hand to hold. The path of light is narrow, but it leads to streets of gold. So take my hand and lift me higher, be my love my desire. Hold me safe, and arms about, take my heart to Higher Ground.

From album entitled Higher Ground
by Barbara Streisand

## The End

.

Steve Josse is an entrepreneur and social activist who lives with his sons in Bend, Oregon. He is co-founder of a model community called *Higher Ground* in Bend.

*One half of the profits from this book go to Higher Ground Community Foundation. Its intent is to build and establish a full fledged community as described in this book.*

To order additional copies of this book, please write to:

New Horizon Book Co.
P.O. Box 8539
Bend, Oregon 97708